SHADOW
OF THE
MINOTAUR

Alan Gibbons is a full time writer and a visiting
speaker and lecturer at schools, colleges and literary
events nationwide, including the major book festivals.
He lives in Liverpool with his wife and four children.

Alan Gibbons has twice been shortlisted for the
Carnegie Medal, with *The Edge* and *Shadow of the
Minotaur* which also won the 'Book I Couldn't Put
Down' category of the Blue Peter Book Awards.

Shadow of the Minotaur is the first part of the Legendeer
Trilogy. *Vampyr Legion* and *Warrors of the Raven*, books
two and three, are also available from Orion.

SHADOW OF THE MINOTAUR

ALAN GIBBONS

Orion
Children's Books

for Joe, Robbie, Rachael and Megan

First published in Great Britain in 2000
as a Dolphin paperback
This paperback edition published 2006
by Orion Children's Books
a division of the Orion Publishing Group Ltd
Orion House
5 Upper St Martin's Lane
London WC2H 9EA

3 5 7 9 10 8 6 4

The Orion Publishing Group's policy is to use papers that
are natural, renewable and recyclable products and
made from wood grown in sustainable forests. The logging
and manufacturing processes are expected to conform to
the environmental regulations of the country of origin.

A catalogue record for this book is available
from the British Library

Printed in Great Britain by
Clays Ltd, St Ives plc

ISBN 978 1 85881 721 7

www.orionbooks.co.uk

Like flies to wanton boys are we to the gods. Aeschylus

What fools we are to live in a generation in which war is a computer game for our children. Tony Benn, MP.

BOOK ONE

The Book of Phoenix

1

The first of the beast's roars almost tore the flesh from his bones. The second, a nerve-splitting bellow that crashed inside his brain, very nearly made him give in before he'd even begun his challenge. He glanced back at the hatch in the door through which he'd just walked and saw the reassuring smile of the dark-eyed girl on the other side. Mustering his own thin smile, he knelt down and picked up the things he'd dropped, a sword with a finely-wrought handle and a ball of strong, thick string.

'You can do this,' he told himself. 'You really can do this.'

But he hadn't convinced his body he could do it. His first attempt at tying the string to the door failed. He was so nervous his fingers just wouldn't work. It was like wearing mittens and trying to knot raw sausages. Taking a deep, shuddering breath he finally managed to pass the string through the hatch and secure it to one of the little bars in the opening. Weighing the sword uncertainly in his hand and letting the string play out behind him, he took his first faltering steps down the dark passageway. The blackness clung to him, trying to crawl inside his skin. The maze of tunnels was everything he'd been expecting – and more. They had the mystery of night, the terror of loneliness. They lay deep beneath the earth, where the sun never shone and the fresh wind never blew, and the silence there was heavy. The air was clogged with a choking animal musk. The walls of the tunnel by the entrance were smooth and regular, built from huge blocks of stone. But as he penetrated deeper into the gloom, he noticed a change. The walls were worn and they were slippery with something thick and slimy. Blood maybe. He flinched then walked on, his feet thudding dully in the cold, still air. Those echoing footsteps shook the close, uncomfortable blackness that clutched at him like a hand. No more than fifty paces from the door the tunnel branched in half a dozen different directions.

He moved forward, unrolling the ball of thread as he went, and stopped. He was still considering his options when he heard the beast again. This time the sound was a low, throaty growl. It was closer, and moving purposefully towards him.

'It's stalking me.'

In the darkness he stumbled and reached out to steady himself. The moment his hand came into contact with the cold stone surface, he recoiled in horror. It was blood all right. There was no mistaking its greasy slide. The walls were slippery with the stuff. The stone floor too. That wasn't all; there were splintered bones, matted hair, gobbets of torn flesh. The tunnels were a slaughterhouse.

'Ugh!'

He immediately wished he hadn't given in so readily to his feeling of disgust. His voice resounded loudly through the tunnels, inviting the beast to attack.

'Now it knows,' he murmured. 'It knows where I am.'

As if to confirm the fact, the beast bellowed through the passageways, mad with rage and hunger. This time the noise was so loud and so shattering that everything around him seemed on the verge of coming apart. The dust began to fall in fine spirals from the ceiling. It was out there in the darkness, snorting and panting, preparing to charge.

'What are you waiting for? Why don't you just do it?'

His breath was coming in troubled gasps. He gripped the sword tightly and edged forward. That's when he noticed a change in the lighting of the tunnel. A shaft of hazy light slanted onto him from above. He looked up and saw a face gazing down at him, the sympathetic face of the girl who had handed him the sword and the ball of string.

'The beast is coming,' she said.

'I know.'

He felt the urge to crouch down, his arms wrapped round himself in a feeble attempt at protection. Now the blackness had a voice.

'Keep down,' it was saying. 'Be small, boy.'

He needed little encouragement. He would have crawled inside himself if that was possible.

But forward he went. And still he played out the thread, marking his route back to the door. Whatever else, he knew he had to hold on to the ball of string. It was his lifeline.

'Where are you?' he whispered under his breath, but there was no answer. The beast wasn't about to give itself away that easily.

Several minutes passed and in that time the beast didn't so much as take a heavy breath. It knew its game, and the game was cat and mouse.

He passed on glancing first ahead, then behind, unsure from which direction the onslaught would come. And the deeper he went into the tunnels the more confused he became. The blackness was tickling his skin, teasing him. Or was that just fear? Where was he? Had he started his approach from the left or the right? Was he moving towards the entrance or away from it? Every one of the passages had the same stone construction and every one of them was worn. Perhaps by the beast, rubbing its horns, or its brawny shoulders against the slippery walls. On he went, bits of bone occasionally crunching under his feet. Once he even kicked a skull, sending it rolling ahead of him. He imagined the bleached, gaping grin and the eye sockets looking up at him, staring their darkness into his soul and sending a rush of fright down his spine.

'Come on,' he hissed. 'Show yourself, for goodness' sake.'

But the sound just hung in the heavy black void, then died away. Savage and untamed as it was, the beast was no dumb animal. It was part-human, and its thinking half was proving both wily and calculating.

It was a dangerous thing, this monster that thought.

'Where are you?'

Leaving the stinking closeness of one of the smaller tunnels, he found himself at a junction in the maze. Then, as he looked around, his heart lurched. He had just tripped over the thread that marked his own path. The string lay criss-crossed over itself.

'I'm going round in circles,' he said in dismay, and his voice rebounded in the chill tunnels. He peered into each of the passageways that led off from the junction. Ignoring the one where the thread lay accusingly on the floor, he made his way down a second tunnel. This one sloped gradually downward.

It was getting colder and the stone floor was oily with puddles of foul water. Dimly shining globs of something unspeakable floated on their dull surfaces. Touching the walls earlier had turned his stomach. He had no intention of making the same mistake with the floor.

Something stirred. A rat? He had never dreamed that he would ever wish for a rat, but just then he would have taken a hundred of the things, rather than the lumbering form waiting for him in the darkness. Hooves scraped on the floor. The sound was made by something big and powerful. This was no rat.

Then he heard the breathing. Slow and steady, calculated and unhurried, a predator's breathing. It had hunted before, yes, and killed too. The thought made his legs weak and rubbery. He turned a corner and found himself at yet another junction, from which more passageways spread like the spokes of a wheel.

'This could go on forever.'

Perhaps the beast shared his feeling that the pursuit had gone on long enough, because it chose that moment to make its move. There was a scraping sound in the gloom, the loudest yet.

He spun round. Framed in the half-light of one opening, the beast was pawing the ground.

'I'm not scared.'

It wasn't true. What's more, the beast knew. His quavering voice settled on the air, painting a picture of his mounting fear. He was clutching the sword's hilt the way a drowning man clings to a piece of driftwood. For comfort. For survival. And, for the first time, he felt its weight. It made his arm shake. His strength was draining away. He tried to grip the hilt with both hands, steadying his weapon.

'Come on then, what are you waiting for?'

But still the beast stood in the archway, pawing at the floor. It was bigger than a man. It stood almost three metres tall and was massively built with slabs of muscle on its chest and shoulders. Below the waist it was bull-like. It had a swinging tail and mud-splattered hooves. Or was it mud? Above the waist it was a man except, that is, for the head. And what a head! The muzzle was huge and when it opened it revealed the sharp, curved teeth, not of a bull but of a big cat. They were the fangs of a lion or tiger, made for ripping flesh. Its eyes were yellow and blazed unflinchingly through the murk. Then there were the great horns, glinting and sharp, curving from its monstrous brow. Thick and muscular as the neck was, it seemed barely able to support such a fearsome head, and strained visibly under the impossible weight.

'Oh my—'

The beast stepped out from the tunnel, and the boy actually took a few steps back. It was as if his soul had crept out of his body and was tugging at him, begging him to get away. In the sparse light shed from the gratings in the ceiling, the beast looked even more hideous. There was the sweat for a start, standing out in gleaming beads on that enormous neck and shoulders.

But that wasn't all. The creature was smeared from head to foot with filth and dried blood. It was every inch a killer. The beast began to stamp forward, its hooves clashing on the stone floor. It raised its head, the horns scraping on the ceiling, and gave a bellow that seemed to crush the air.

'I can't do this . . .'

He fell back, scrambling over obstacles on the floor, and fled. That's when he realized he'd dropped the ball of string. His lifeline had gone.

'Oh no!'

The beast was charging head down.

Got to get out of here!

In his mind's eye, he could see himself impaled on the points of those evil-looking horns, his legs pedalling feebly in the air, his head snapped back, his eyes growing pale and lifeless.

Suddenly, he was running for his life, skidding on the slimy floor.

'Help me!'

He saw the startled brown eyes of the girl above the grating.

'Don't run!' she cried. 'Fight. You must fight.'

He was almost dying of shame. This wasn't supposed to happen. He wasn't meant to lose and there weren't meant to be witnesses to his defeat.

'Fight,' she repeated. 'It's the way of things.'

The way of things. That's right, he was meant to stand and fight. It was in his nature as a hero. But he couldn't. Not against *that*.

'Please,' he begged, turning his face away from the girl in shame, 'somebody help me.'

The beast was careering through the tunnels, crashing, bellowing thundering through the maze. Its charge was hot, furious, unstoppable. It was almost on him.

Get me out of here!

'That's it,' he cried, throwing down his sword, 'I've had enough. Game over!'

2

Ripping off the mask and gloves, Phoenix bent double gulping down air like it had been rationed. The dank half-light of the tunnels was replaced by the welcome glow from an Anglepoise lamp in his father's study. He glanced at the score bracelet on his wrist. It registered total defeat: **000000**. For a few moments everything was spinning, the claws of the game digging into the flesh of the here and now. Then his surroundings became reassuringly familiar.

He was out.

*It **was** a game!*

'Well?' his dad asked, 'What do you think?'

'Mind-blowing,' Phoenix panted. 'It was all so real. It was like another world. I mean, I *was* Theseus. I went into the palace of the tyrant-king Minos. I could actually touch the stone columns, feel the heat of the braziers, smell the incense.'

He knew he was gushing, babbling like a little kid, but he didn't care. 'The king's daughter Ariadne helped me and she wasn't just an image on a screen. She was a real girl. Then I actually came face to face with the Minotaur. It was really happening. I believed it.' He shivered. 'Still do.'

'Oh, I could tell how convincing it was,' said Dad, enjoying the mixture of excitement and fear in his son's voice. 'You were screaming your silly head off by the end. I bet your mother thought I was killing you in here.'

Phoenix blushed then, beginning to control his breathing at last, he picked up the mask and gloves and traced the attached wires back to the computer where images of the labyrinth were still flashing away on the screen.

9

'It really was just a game?'

Dad pushed his seat back and gave a superior smile.

'That's all. Just a very sophisticated piece of software, hooked up to an even more sophisticated piece of hardware.'

Scared as he had been, Phoenix didn't want it to be a game. He wanted it to be real. Real and vibrant as the old legends had always seemed to him. He fingered the soft texture of the amazing gloves and mask that had created the illusion. 'And you get to play with all this great stuff for a living?'

'I certainly do. And there's a lot more to come. To quote my boss, Mr Glen Reede: *This is only stage one in the development of the ultimate game.*'

Phoenix stared at the screen and the figure of the Minotaur. Is that what he'd been afraid of? That ridiculous cartoon-strip monster blinking on the screen.

'Maybe now you'll quit complaining about moving to Brownleigh.'

That was asking a bit much. When Dad gave up his job at Compu-soft and accepted the lucrative offer from Magna-com, he'd fulfilled a lifelong dream. Only it was *his* lifelong dream. Phoenix and his mother had hated moving out of London, away from family and friends, especially when it meant re-settling in a one-eyed backwater halfway between Dullsville and Nowhere. Life's the game, thought Phoenix, a boring game of patience.

'We could have stayed in London,' Phoenix argued. 'After all, you're working from home. What was wrong with the house we had?'

'Where do you want to start?' Dad asked. 'The noise, the pollution, the rat race, the crime.'

Phoenix shook his head. The city had got Dad down, but he could keep his peace and quiet.

Brownleigh was a dump. No cinema, no sports centre, no railway station. There was nothing at all to do, and when it came to escaping the boredom, the buses to the nearest big town stopped at 10 o'clock. Phoenix was still trying to work out what people did round here. Maybe they took a chair out onto the pavement so they could watch the traffic lights change!

He'd gone from a city that never sleeps to a town that never wakes up. That was why he couldn't forgive his dad. London was what Phoenix craved – something big and important – and Dad had taken him away from it. Dad hadn't just pulled out of the rat race, he'd just about pulled out of life.

'Anyway,' said Dad, unplugging the mask and gloves from the phone socket in the PC, 'We're here now so you'd better make the best of it.'

Phoenix watched Dad carefully wrapping the experimental game equipment.

'There is something I don't understand,' he said.

'And that is?'

'You've produced this game so quickly. I thought it took months to get something like this off the ground, years even.'

'It does,' Dad agreed, 'with the usual technology. But this is several steps beyond the norm. Half the work's been done for me already. *More* than half. The company has developed a basic computer environment. It's so flexible that you can program in each new story line for a game in weeks. I take the story line lines your mum comes up with and, with a bit of help from me, the software just seems to grow into it.'

Phoenix frowned at the mention of Mum's story lines. Mum and Phoenix were two of a kind. They both had dreams, they both had a sense of destiny. Her dream was to be a writer – any kind of writer. She'd been trying forever to get published. First a romantic novel, then some poems, finally a short story competition, but she never got anywhere. She actually kept the rejection slips, as if they were some sort of stepping stone to success! Writing was just another disappointment, along with Brownleigh – and Dad.

Dad had no idea what was going on in Phoenix's head, and carried on regardless. 'I don't even need to come up with half the graphics. The images have already been stored in the computer's memory. I'm little more than a scene-shifter. I bring ready-made images and story lines into focus. Money for

11

old rope, really. Glen Reede's the one who created this, he's the genius. I tell you, when this comes out at the end of next month, Reede's going to change the face of computer games.'

'Did you say the end of next month?'

'That's right,' said Dad. 'The advertising and marketing is already done. That's why I'm working all the hours God sends. It's one heck of a deadline, but Reede will make sure it's met. You can bet your bottom dollar on it. He's a giant. I just can't understand why I haven't come across his name before. No articles in *Computers and Computing*, no reputation to speak of. I'm guessing he's American, but there's no biog. on the Internet. He's come out of nowhere. Still, who cares so long as he's ready to have me on board.'

Phoenix smiled as Dad locked the game gear away. There was something very odd about Dad of all people creating games about heroes. Anybody less like a hero would be hard to imagine. He looked like the original computer geek, complete with untidy red hair, patchy, unkempt beard, corduroy trousers and a lumberjack shirt that strained to contain his thickening waist. There had been a time, in his early twenties, when he'd been a promising tennis player, but that seemed an awfully long time ago. Phoenix wasn't sure whether the old man tried to look like a nerd, or whether it just came naturally. Whatever his intentions, he managed to drive Mum mad with his eccentric, slobbish behaviour. He could have featured in a sitcom – Dads Behaving Madly. But he must have something going for him. He'd been head-hunted by this Glen Reede character, the multi-millionaire boss of Magna-com who had offered him a small fortune to join the company as a creator of mass-market computer games.

They'd done up the cottage with the 'golden hello' Dad had got from Magna-com.

That's it. He was a computer hero!

'So tell me,' Dad continued, 'as a fourteen-year old, you're a member of our target audience. Will it sell?'

'Sell! It'll go like hot cakes. A game you can actually get into—'

12

'Hey, that'd make a good advertising line: *The computer game you can **really** get into.*' Dad scribbled it down on a spiral-bound notepad. 'What about the mask and the gloves? Not too sweaty?'

'Not at all,' Phoenix replied. 'They're dead comfortable. The material is really soft. It's almost like a second skin.'

'That's the idea,' Dad explained. 'It's got to be comfortable and easy to get on and off, or the kids will think it's just too much trouble and stick with their old games.'

'Not much chance of that,' said Phoenix, still unable to take his eyes off the monitor screen. 'I mean, it felt like I was really moving around. The graphics were amazing.'

'As good as reality?'

'Better.' Phoenix blushed as he realized what he had said. 'You know, it's true. Stories can be better than real life.' He paused then, unable to resist the temptation to have a dig. 'Especially when real life means Brownleigh.'

Dad ignored the last remark. 'I'm not sure all kids are like you, mind. How many teenagers have their noses in a book of Greek myths half the evening? But a computer game on the other hand – this time they won't have their *noses* in a book, they'll have their whole selves in the story. That's what's been wrong with all these computer games so far. No matter how good the graphics are, you always know that you're in a game. But if you can convince your player that he is actually inside it, *living it*, then you're onto a winner.'

'I guess so,' said Phoenix, wilting slightly under Dad's tidal wave of enthusiasm. 'But it's got to be as good as the one I've just played. It's got to be a match for the real world.'

'Exactly,' Dad interrupted. 'Not so much virtual reality as *parallel reality*. That's what I'm doing now, getting rid of any fuzziness, any sense that this is an electronic entertainment. You can't get most kids off their Playstations now. But when this comes out, forget life. Everybody will have one in their living room. The game will be everything. In six weeks it will be a household name. It'll make us a fortune.'

'You're right there,' said Phoenix. 'It's an amazing

experience. I didn't just *see* the labyrinth, I was there. I could feel it, I could smell it. That's what made it so scary. How did you do that?'

Dad scratched his chin.

'To tell you the truth, I don't really know. You've got to remember, I'm only one part of a team. I play with the jigsaw. Other people provide most of the pieces.'

'Funny sort of team if you never get together,' said Phoenix. 'You've really never met anybody else from the company?'

'No, I haven't,' said Dad. 'Reede contracts everything out to people like me working from home. Maybe he doesn't want anybody getting a complete picture of the game. Whatever his reasons, I've only been given the top two levels, nine and ten, to do. I don't even know the names of the people doing the lower levels. It doesn't really matter. I just take the story lines, match them with the animated action I get and send them in. Magna-com does the rest, and does it at astonishing speed. These Greek myths seemed as good a place to start as any.'

They certainly were for Mum and Phoenix, who prided themselves on their Greek roots. Most of their relatives had settled in London, but they still exchanged Christmas cards with the odd uncle or aunt on some Aegean island. That was something else Dad had taken them away from when they left the capital – their past.

'Great plots, great monsters, great heroes,' Dad ran on, 'and in you and your mum I've got a couple of experts around if I need to pick anybody's brains. As for this feel-around technology, I don't know how Reede does it myself.'

Mum popped her head round the door. 'Are you two ready for something to eat? You've been stuck in here for two hours already.'

Phoenix glanced outside. It was true. Dusk was gathering over the ancient yew trees at the end of the lane. It was something he'd noticed about a good computer game. It seemed to be able to pull time out of shape, mould it and remake it the way a potter does a vase on the wheel. It could turn hours into minutes and minutes into hours. Phoenix had been known to spend a whole day at the screen, even begrudging the time spent on meals. Like most kids, he'd perfected the *just-five-more-minutes* routine. As he got up from his chair, he found himself thinking how grateful he was that he'd taken after Mum when it came to looks. In sharp contrast to his red-haired, pear-shaped dad, she was tall, slim and dark.

Mediterranean-gorgeous, as one of his mates back in London used to say.

'Aren't you shutting down?' Mum asked.

'No need,' said Dad. 'I'll eat and come straight back on. Deadlines, Christina.'

'Oh, you're not going to be on it all night, are you?' asked Mum.

Dad shrugged.

'One of these days,' she said, leading the way into the kitchen. 'We'll have a life. Work, work, work, that's all you care about. Go on, shut down. Just for an hour.'

Dad gave way. As he shut down the screen was filled with a sequence of numbers.

'What's all that?' asked Phoenix. It intrigued him, like the first part of a puzzle. 'There's nothing wrong, is there?'

'Beats me,' Dad admitted. 'Some sort of encrypted message, though you'd have to be an expert to crack it. One of Glen Reede's little secrets.'

But wasn't Dad an expert? Phoenix frowned. Here was something he didn't understand and he was willing to just gloss over it.

'So, what about the characters?' Dad asked over the kitchen table a few minutes later. 'Do they work?'

'Yes, I think so,' said Phoenix. It was hard to take him seriously with strands of cheese sauce dangling from his beard. 'But I've only played one episode of the legend, remember. Theseus is right. And Princess Ariadne, she makes Lara Croft look like a bag lady!'

'Oh, by the way, Reede has just released the title—'

'*The Legendeer,*' Mum said absent-mindedly, her eyes on the road outside and her mind a world away.

15

'Now how did you know that?' gasped Dad.

Mum started, as if wrenched out of a magical dreamtime.

'I've no idea,' she said, troubled by her own intuition. 'You must have mentioned it sometime.'

'No, that's impossible. It was embargoed. I—'

'Oh, does it matter?' snapped Mum.

They exchanged hostile glares. For some reason it mattered a lot.

'Anyway,' Phoenix interrupted in an effort to prevent a row. '*The Legendeer* is great. You were lucky getting the Theseus and Perseus levels to do.'

'Why's that?'

'Well, they're both boy heroes, about my age. I reckon they'll appeal to that target audience you're always going on about, teenagers.'

Dad frowned. 'Boy heroes, eh? You don't think they look a bit too old, do you?'

Mum smiled. 'It's a bit late to think of it now. Honestly, they put you in charge of developing the story line for the game, and you don't even read the source books properly. You're such a philistine, John.'

'Oh, come off it,' Dad retorted, 'It's a computer game, not a novel. I skip all the boring stuff.'

Mum raised her eyes. 'Boring stuff indeed! This is my Greek heritage you're talking about; truths that speak to me down a hundred generations. These are some of the greatest stories ever told. They're about reaching manhood, about young men growing up and proving themselves, surviving in a hostile world. They're about great friendship and crushing betrayal—'

Noticing the look of amusement on Dad's face, she faltered. He never seemed to take her seriously. Not her writing, not her ancestry. Maybe that's what she resented so much. She believed in the magic and mystery of things, the spaces between what could be explained, whereas Dad reduced everything to a series of provable facts.

'Besides,' she said abruptly. 'They've got two of the best

monsters in the business, Medusa and the Minotaur. That's what got you hooked in the first place.'

'I'll make a few adjustments then,' said Dad. 'I take it you won't mind being my guinea pig, Phoenix. You'll be prepared to play both levels as we make the finishing touches?'

'Are you kidding?' cried Phoenix. 'I'd love it.'

That's when he remembered the yellow eyes of the Minotaur and its ferocious roar. He'd love it all right, just so long as it didn't get *too* real.

3

But it was going to get real, and sooner than either Phoenix or Dad dreamed. There was a message hidden among those bewildering sequences of numbers, a coded signal that might have made John Graves think twice about carrying on working for Glen Reede at all. A dizzying parade of threes, sixes and nines was flashing across the screen as the computer shut down.

*Did you enjoy your time in the labyrinth, my brave young Theseus? Did you feel the thrill of the dark, the enticing smell of your own death? How lucky you are to be able to come in on the most advanced levels. They're reserved for the players most deserving of a glorious demise. But you, you insignificant microbe, you get to face the greatest perils. What an oddity that your father is the most able programmer I've got, so you start at the top. Don't get over confident, though. I'm giving you a taster of the game, that's all. It is pathetic, really pathetic to watch **you**, a mere boy, trying to stand up to my magnificent beast. I might let you tread the slimy stones of his realm a little longer, teasing you. There are no free rides in this game.*

*   I promise you – this is just the beginning.*

4

Legends are not just one of my interests, they're my life.

Where did that come from?

Phoenix shook his head. Where *on Earth* did that come from, and why did he have to go and blurt it out in front of the whole class? Was he trying to make himself look a complete idiot? If he knew Steve Adams – and unfortunately it was one of his burdens in life that he did know him – he'd pay for that little outburst. What was he thinking of? It was one thing to swallow what Mum said about legends speaking to them down a hundred generations, and spend hours poring over dusty old volumes full of spoilt, cruel gods, courageous heroes and fabulous, blood-drenched monsters. It was quite another to show himself up in class like that. This was the world he had to live in, not some never-never land of temples and demons. That's what he'd done though, he'd made a complete idiot of himself halfway through double English. Look at me, the new kid, I'm after the Nerd of the Year award.

And this is what he said to earn it: *Don't you understand, Miss? These myths. They're not just stories. They're real. They show us as heroes. They're our true nature.*

That's what came of getting so wrapped up in Dad's *Legendeer* project. Phoenix had played the game three times in the last week and he'd started quite fancying himself as one of those heroes. Unfortunately, the very thought of Phoenix as a hero had Adams and his idiot hangers-on cackling fit to burst. Most of the boys in Phoenix's class wouldn't admit to reading at all. It didn't do much for your street cred. It was seen as a girl thing. And they definitely didn't believe that what they read

19

was real. So what did Phoenix do? He actually announced to the whole world that books were *better* than life, that he saw himself as a Theseus or a Herakles.

With his flesh still creeping from the embarrassment of that awful afternoon, Phoenix dashed out of the school gates like a bat out of Hell. It was in danger of bringing on one of his sick headaches. They were the bane of his life. They would come from nowhere and last a few hours, completely draining him. He had had all sorts of hospital tests but the doctors had never been able to explain them. Or treat them. With the passing years, the family had learned to live with the problem. Headaches and embarrassment – what a life! Phoenix remembered the score bracelet he'd worn in the game. For the second time in as many days it would have registered the fatal numbers: **000000.**

A loser with knobs on.

Even being a loser wouldn't have been so bad, but Phoenix suffered from something else. An exaggerated sense of his own importance. All his life he had had this idea nagging away at the back of his mind.

I've got a purpose in life. Something big.

It just made the boring reality even worse. *Something big—*

He snorted. 'Sure, something like keeping out of Adams' way.'

The 221 bus was waiting at the bus stop. If I catch this one, Phoenix thought, maybe I'll be gone before he gets out of school. He sat watching the jostling groups of kids getting on. It soon became obvious the driver wasn't going to move off until the bus was full.

'Oh, come on,' said Phoenix. 'Go!'

But the kids kept piling on board. Eventually, he pulled a book out and started reading. It was the Greek myths, of course. Phoenix shivered as he remembered his performance in class. Geek myths would be more like it. After a couple of minutes he heard a tap on the window. It was Laura.

'Save me a place.'

She flashed her pass and shoved her way down the bus.

'You were miles away,' she said.

Miles? Centuries was more like it. In his mind he was already treading the labyrinth again. He hoped Dad would let him have another go that evening. He didn't care how scary the labyrinth was, he'd get that stupid Minotaur yet. He'd been talking to Mum, working out his moves, and he was sure he had a plan. Brain, not brawn, would conquer the beast. At least at home, in the privacy of the study, he could be a hero.

'Go on,' she said, digging him playfully in the ribs. 'What were you thinking about?'

Laura Osibona's friendship was about the only thing that made living in Brownleigh half-bearable. Her brown, almost black eyes sparkled as she fingered the book lying half-open on the seat.

'What's this, Phoenix?' she asked. 'Let's have a look. Oh dear.'

She pouted with mock disapproval.

'Not those ghastly beasties again.'

She was teasing, but Phoenix found it a lot easier to take from her than from Steve Adams and his mates. They used humour like a knife, twisting it until they drew blood. Laura, on the other hand, didn't have a cruel bone in her body.

Phoenix glanced at the book's drab olive-green cover, and remembered the clash of the Minotaur's hooves on the floor of the labyrinth. If only she knew what lurked inside those pages. Phoenix had never really read for pleasure. He read to immerse himself in worlds that seemed as real as the one he had to grow up in. Now the game was opening the door to them. Did he dare tell Laura? But Dad had sworn him to secrecy on the whole project.

Commercial confidentiality.

'Yes Laura, those ghastly beasties.'

It was a relief to talk to her, to make fun of his fears, cut his demons down to size. Much as he'd enjoyed it, the encounter with the Minotaur had spooked him good style. The only reason he felt ready to play again was because Dad's finger would be on the off button.

21

'*The Concise Dictionary of Myths and Legends*,' Laura read. 'Light reading, eh?'

She flicked through the pages.

'He looks like you,' she said, showing him the illustration of one of the legendary heroes.

'That's Theseus,' said Phoenix. 'Do you really think he looks like me?'

'Spitting image,' Laura confirmed.

Then she was nudging him along the seat.

'Well, are you going to let me sit down, or what?'

Between him and his school holdall, Phoenix was hogging the whole seat.

'Budge up, Phoenix.'

Phoenix! It wasn't just his monsters the other kids laughed at. He was even a victim of his own name. Didn't Mum and Dad know how important it was to fit in? Adams was having a field day with it. Bundling his holdall to the floor, Phoenix moved over to the window.

'Oh, great!'

'What's up?'

'Look who's getting on.'

Adams had just appeared with his usual bunch of cronies. The gang leader was lean and tall. A wolf in wolf's clothing.

'Take no notice,' said Laura.

Phoenix sighed. 'Easier said than done. They're staring.'

Laura took the news calmly.

'Let them. They're only jealous.'

'So they've got something to be jealous of, have they?'

Laura dug him in the ribs. 'Now that would be telling.'

Phoenix found himself smiling. They'd hit it off right from the start. Just when he was cursing his luck at ending up in such a tedious little town, full of no-hopers like Adams, Laura had arrived to make his day. Her best friend Kathy had been off so there had been a spare seat next to her. Kathy never got her place back. Phoenix and Laura had been inseparable since then. It set tongues wagging of course, but it didn't really bother him. They were meant to be friends and that was that.

22

But if they were friends, shouldn't he—? No, Dad would kill him. Oh, what the heck, this was too big to keep to himself. He gave Laura his in-confidence look.

'If I tell you something,' he began, 'do you promise to keep it to yourself?'

'Of course.'

Phoenix knew Dad would kill him, but he was dying to tell somebody about *The Legendeer*.

'I mean it,' he said. 'You can't tell a soul, not even Kathy.'

'I promise, you creep.'

Phoenix glanced at the kids around them. They were too busy with the latest gossip to take much notice.

'You know my dad makes computer games?'

'Yes, you told me.'

'Well, you should see the latest thing he's doing.'

'Why, is it good?'

'Good? It's amazing.'

Phoenix leaned forward conspiratorially.

'You know there are these games where you can wear a glove instead of using a control pad?'

'Sure. And you can get those Virtual Reality helmet things.'

'Well,' Phoenix told her excitedly. 'Dad's company has just come up with something even better. It's state of the art. It feels like you're right inside the game.'

Laura looked intrigued.

'What game?'

'It's called *The Legendeer*.'

Just mentioning the game caused a curious tugging at the coat-tails of his memory. Like Mum, he was beginning to think he'd heard the name before.

'Legends, eh? That should be right down your street.'

'It is. I've been helping Dad with the story line. I get to play Theseus going to the palace of King Minos to fight the Minotaur.' He knew he was gushing, but he didn't care. *The Legendeer* was something you just couldn't oversell. 'The game's incredible. King Minos' daughter Princess Ariadne helps me kill the beast. She looks as real as you or me. I'm talking flesh and blood, totally 3-D. You'd swear there were real people in the game.'

'Could I play it?'

Phoenix frowned.

'I'm afraid not. It's at the experimental stage. It's sort of secret.'

It was Laura's turn to frown.

'So, if you won't let me have a go, why are you telling me about it?'

Phoenix was beginning to wonder himself.

'I had to tell somebody. It's really cool. You don't just see the monster's lair. You can smell it, you can feel it.'

'That's impossible.'

'Not any more.'

Laura put her head on one side.

'You're having me on.'

'I'm not,' said Phoenix. 'Honestly I'm not. It's about the most exciting thing I've ever done.'

'Prove it then.'

'How do you mean?'

'I mean,' Laura said pointedly, 'if you want me to swallow this big secret of yours, you've got to let me play it.'

Phoenix was wondering how to get out of the hole he'd dug for himself, when Adams and his gang appeared in front of him.

'Hey, Free Knickers,' Adams smirked. 'That was a corker you came out with this afternoon. Nobody would believe me when I told them what a freak of nature you are. Now they've found out for themselves. Seen any ghosties and ghoulies lately? Had any books come to life? Go on Free Knickers, give us all a laugh.'

'The name,' Phoenix growled, 'is Phoenix.'

He could feel that twinge of headache developing into the familiar band of pain that had plagued him all his life. The slightest little thing could set it off, strong sunlight, nerves, loud noise. Then it was heat rashes and headaches. He'd often spent hours lying on the couch in a darkened room with a

24

damp cloth on his forehead, listening to Mum turning away his friends with talk of, *one of his heads.*

'Phoenix, Free Knickers, whatever. What sort of name is that, anyway? Your folks hippies or something?'

Phoenix stiffened. That's exactly what Dad was, a throwback to the days when people wore their hair long and slopped around in tie-dyed shirts.

There was actually a pair of blue-tinted John Lennon glasses in a drawer somewhere. Laura was squeezing Phoenix's arm, making a silent plea for restraint.

'Don't rise to it.'

But Phoenix was stung. He was touchy about his nerdy little dad, the redhaired geek who used to turn up at his primary school wearing this giant, floppy ski hat. What an embarrassment that was! That's right, Dad *had* been a bit of a hippy, only twenty years too late.

'You shut your mouth, Adams!'

'Or what?'

Or nothing. Phoenix was angry. He wasn't suicidal.

'Leave it, Phoenix,' said Laura. 'Here's our stop.'

But Adams didn't know how to let go. He was like a dog with a bone. He was going to chew and chew until he got to the marrow.

'Just look at his face,' said Adams laughing. 'Lighten up, Free Knickers. No need to get uptight on me.'

Phoenix watched the mocking glint in Adams' eye and he hated it. He hated the reminder that he wasn't special after all, that he didn't fight demons. Not real ones. He hated Adams for being a common or garden small-town bully. He hated him, full stop.

'Take your hands off me.'

'Don't be so touchy, Free Knickers my old mate. Just sit there like a good boy while I have a word with the lovely Laura.'

Suddenly, Phoenix was seeing everything through a red mist. Good boy! Good *boy*. Adams' face, so cruel and taunting. His friends, urging him on with their jibes and laughter. Then

Adams was pushing against Laura, trying to make room for himself on the seat.

It's not that he really fancied her. Adams was quite a racist, and used to pick on Laura as one of the few black kids in school, but if he could use her to get at Phoenix he would. Phoenix glanced outside at the pavement. The bus was slowing down as it approached his and Laura's stop.

'You don't mind, do you?'

Adams taunted Phoenix, his thin lips curled. A smile should be a mark of friendship. With him, it was a weapon, as sharp and effective as a scalpel.

'No, of course you don't.'

Phoenix listened to the arrogance in Adams' voice. He was cock of the school, a boy used to getting his own way, even with the teachers who he was expert at winding up. So, Phoenix told himself, thinks he's fireproof, does he? His neck was burning with shame and fury, and the headache was building.

I can't let him get away with this.

'I was thinking, Laura, why don't you ditch old Free Knickers and come to town with me? Me and the lads will show you a good time.'

The bus was stopping. He couldn't let Adams get away with it, but what could he do? In the event, he didn't do anything. Laura had it in hand.

'Forget it, Steve,' she said, tossing her dreadlocked hair. 'Mum doesn't want me dating anybody at my age. Besides, you're the last boy I'd go out with.' A pause, then she was trying to get up. 'Excuse me, please. This is our stop.'

Phoenix imagined himself crashing his fist into Adams' leering face, but that wasn't his style. He *read* about fights or engaged in them in his on-screen battles with the demons. That was the best sort of fighting, the kind you could stop at the touch of the off-button.

As the gang stepped back, he followed Laura meekly off the bus, ignoring the sly kick in the calf, and burning with humiliation at the insults being shouted behind him.

'Just look at him,' sneered Adams. 'Hiding behind Laura's skirt.'

Hiding! Phoenix didn't want to hide. He didn't want to hide or run ever again. He'd sampled danger in the game. It made him think maybe he did have a destiny after all.

'I should have thumped him,' Phoenix grumbled as they reached the pelican crossing.

'And what good would that do?' asked Laura. 'You can't take on the whole gang. I can handle Steve. I've been doing it for years. I'm not some damsel in distress and you're no knight in shining armour.'

But I could be, thought Phoenix. If I mastered this game, I really could be.

5

'Is that you, Phoenix?'

'Yuh.'

Mum met him in the hallway. She put the ring-bind folder she was carrying down on one of the piles of marking stacked along the wall.

'Uh oh, what's wrong?'

Phoenix could hear Dad tapping away at the keyboard. It was getting to be the usual routine; Mum at her school work or her writing on the kitchen table, Dad in the study trying to get the game right. The one thing they never seemed to do was talk to each other. Phoenix wished they could give up work and get a life.

'Nothing's wrong.'

'Don't give me that. What's happened?'

'I told you, nothing.'

'It was Steve Adams again, wasn't it?'

Phoenix nodded.

'He didn't hurt you, did he?'

'Not exactly.'

'Then what exactly?'

Phoenix hated having to tell her. It meant reliving the humiliation.

'He kind of shoved us around. Me and Laura.'

'I knew it. He's a bad one, that Adams.'

Phoenix looked away. Tell me something I don't know.

'So, how many of them were there this time?'

'Four.'

'I'm going to have a word with that school. We don't have that sort of behaviour at mine.'

Phoenix thought it was hardly surprising. She taught ten-year-olds. He didn't want her causing trouble though.

'No, Mum,' he pleaded. 'Don't.'

Didn't she know that would only make things worse?

'Well, we've got to do something.'

Why? When they lived in London they had a neighbour who used to play his music at all hours. And at full volume too. Dad went round once and the neighbour started getting heavy.

'Want to make something of it?' he'd asked. Dad didn't.

And now, Phoenix thought, I'm following in the old man's footsteps. Big ideas, but no action.

'You just tell me if it happens again,' Mum said.

Phoenix gave a half-nod. It didn't mean a thing, but it seemed to satisfy Mum.

'What's up?' asked Dad, wandering in from the study. 'Were you two arguing?'

'Nothing you need to worry about,' said Mum. 'A bit of bullying. I'll handle it. You get on with your work and leave the real world to me.'

Dad glanced at Phoenix. His face said *Ouch*.

'Pop in and see me when you've finished here, son.'

After another five minutes of ear-bending from Mum, Phoenix escaped to the study.

'You OK?' Dad asked.

'Yes, I'm fine.'

He would have liked Dad to listen to his problems now they were out in the open, tell him how he'd handled this sort of stuff when he was in his teens. But Dad was no great shakes in the Man-to-Man Talk Department.

He carried on as if nothing had happened.

'Good. I've got something to show you.'

Dad was almost trembling with excitement. Part of Phoenix shared the thrill of a new toy, but another part of him hung back, still annoyed that Dad didn't want to listen to his problems.

'There!'

Dad was holding up what looked like a very flimsy diving suit.

'What is it?'

'Can't you guess?'

Phoenix shook his head.

'Here,' said Dad, jabbing a finger at the balaclava-like mask at the top of the suit. 'Recognize this?'

'It's the helmet I wore to play the game.'

'And these?'

Dad flapped the gloves at him. Phoenix was catching on.

'You mean it's a Virtual Reality suit?'

Dad winked.

'Better than that. We've created a *Parallel Reality* suit.'

Phoenix felt the material. It was just like the mask and gloves. A second skin. Except this time, it was an all-over skin. It was bound to make the illusion even more convincing.

'*You* made this?'

'Well, I e-mailed the idea to Magna-com and this came back.'

'When did it come?'

'Second post this afternoon. I could hardly believe it. The game is developing by the day.'

Phoenix stared at the suit.

'But they couldn't come up with something like this so quickly. They must have been working on it already.'

'Oh, I'm sure they were,' said Dad. 'But they're ready to try it out. With luck, this kit will be ready for launch day. It's much more advanced than the first equipment we tried. Want to play guinea pig?'

'What, now?'

Dad chuckled.

'No time like the present.'

Phoenix examined the suit.

'How do I get it on? I can't see any fastenings.'

Dad grinned.

'It took me a while to figure it out. Here.'

30

He guided Phoenix's hands to a barely-visible line down the front of the suit.

'Now, just pull it like you're opening a bag of crisps.'

Phoenix tugged and the suit opened with a barely audible hiss.

'What is it, Velcro?'

'I couldn't work it out myself. It doesn't feel sticky or anything. It's more advanced than Velcro, that's for sure.'

Phoenix put his feet into the suit and pulled it up to his armpits. He slipped his arms in then finally pulled the mask down, snapping it over his jawline.

'How does it feel?'

Phoenix looked around. His mouth and eyes were covered by a very fine gauze.

'I hardly even feel like I'm wearing it. Am I plugged into the PC?'

'Hang on. I'll hook you up now.'

Phoenix heard the purr of the PC as it stirred into life. He strapped on his score bracelet. He couldn't wait to re-enter the world of *The Legendeer*. No way was he going to register the Big Zero this time.

'Right,' said Dad. 'You're all set. Here, you carry on.'

Phoenix loaded the disc. Previously, he had gone straight into the labyrinth. This time it was different. Credits started flashing up on the screen.

Manufactured by: Magna-com International. Dir: Glen Reede.

Marketing: Arcadia Computers.

Copyright: Tartarus Applications.

Clues rolled onto the screen. Teasing signposts to the rules of the game. Phoenix smiled.

All Greek to me?

I don't think so.

The title sequence began. He stared at the screen with a mixture of anxiety and excitement as a horned face appeared. A thrill ran through him. Phoenix watched the strange figure emerge grinning from a boiling cloud. His hair was dark and wiry, streaked with grey. What's more, it came down his forehead to the bridge of his nose in a V-shape. His long, hooked nose was hairy too, and his skin was sunburnt and weather-beaten, scored with wrinkles and crow's feet. Most noticeable of all was his smile, wide, thick-lipped. He was the god of shepherds, prophecy and mischief – Pan. His hoarse, chafing voice scraped in the speakers. 'Welcome, friend, to the world of *The Legendeer.'*

Pan smiled. It was perfect. Phoenix had only played a snippet of the game until now. This was the real thing, complete with introduction and player's guide.

'Hello Pan.'

'Let me introduce you to my domain.'

Our domain, thought Phoenix as a sheer wall of rock rose before him, the summit swathed in mist.

'Behold,' ran the introduction. 'Cloud-dark Olympus. They say it takes an anvil nine days and nine nights to fall from Heaven to Earth.'

'Yeah yeah, I know all this. Get to the game.'

The game! No headaches any more. Phoenix was almost trembling with excitement.

'Far below, my dear disciple,' Pan continued, 'is dismal Tartarus, the land of dead souls. That sad country lies as far below Earth as Heaven stands above it. Do you remember how far, my friend?'

'Of course I remember,' Phoenix replied. 'Nine days and nights as the anvil falls.'

For a split-second he remembered Dad's presence in the room, but so what, he was enjoying himself.

'Your task is simple, player, you must go through the many labours of the hero, march forward through the very jaws of death itself and claim your place on High Olympus in the company of the gods. Are you ready to proceed?'

Phoenix smiled.

'OK Mister Pan, I'm hooked.'

As the screen faded out then back in again, the game's illusion started to suck Phoenix in. He was introduced to a vast mountainside shimmering under a blazing sun, and he wasn't looking at the screen any more. He was there, standing on the sheep-grazed slopes. Pan was present in person, man from the waist up, goat from the waist down. He was dancing on the mountain top, playing the seven-reed Arcadian pipes. And the strangest thought came to Phoenix: *I'm home.*

'Ready, young friend? Select your hero.'

Phoenix looked up. There they were, emblazoned on the sky, the heroes of antiquity: Herakles, Orpheus, Achilles, Jason, Perseus, Theseus. The list went on. They were arranged in groups. All but Perseus and Theseus were slightly faded. They couldn't be accessed.

'Fair enough. I'll take the boy heroes.'

Images of the heroes hovered in front of him. He remembered what Laura had said about the picture in his book. He inspected the heroes closely. Theseus bore him more than a passing resemblance. By touching the floating image, Phoenix selected Theseus.

'Starting at the top,' said Pan. 'Still, there's nothing like ambition. You are now Theseus of Troezen. Your father left you here when you were a baby. He is King Aegeus of Athens. You haven't seen him for fourteen years.'

Just my age, thought Phoenix. The game fits me like a glove.

'Now it is time to claim your birthright,' Pan resumed. 'You are the true and destined heir to the throne of Athens. Follow me, *Prince* Theseus.'

Phoenix – or was it Theseus? – felt that he was being teased. But he was hooked. He started to follow Pan along a dirt path between the cypress trees. The heat haze shimmered. He could actually feel it on his skin. And hear the scrape of the crickets. And smell the sheep on the hillside close by. The illusion was even better than the first time.

Besides the smells and sounds, he could actually taste the dust. Better than real life? No doubt about that.

'And here,' said Pan, springing on to a ledge of rock, 'I must leave you. Welcome to your first challenge.'

He pointed to a huge boulder.

'Roll back this rock and you will discover the tokens by which you will prove your identity to the King of Athens. Your epic journey begins here.'

Phoenix stared at the rock. It was impossible. At least, it should have been, but this was a game, and games are places where miracles can happen. He stepped forward and braced his shoulder against the rock. Straining every muscle, he shoved at the boulder. Nothing. Again, he was struck by the sheer reality of the game. This rock, it was physically there. He took a deep breath and planted his feet down hard on the sun-baked earth. As he heaved again, he felt his shoes sliding and scraping on the ground. This time it was moving. It was gradual at first, then the boulder was rolling steadily towards a steep slope. With a last push, Phoenix sent it bouncing down the hillside. He felt the score bracelet chattering away against his wrist. *I'm scoring.*

He knelt down to examine what was underneath – a pair of sandals and a sword. The ivory hilt of the sword bore the seal of King Aegeus, three entwined serpents. The score bracelet was recording still more points. He was on a roll. He weighed the weapon in his hand, remembering the grim trial ahead, his entry into the labyrinth to face the Minotaur.

His mind was concentrating on the beast that haunted the dark tunnels when a hand fell on his shoulder. His chest cramped in the agony of fear.

It's the game. It won't let go.

Suddenly, he knew what a heart attack must feel like. His head was pounding and his blood was on fire. He was looking at Dad's study through a boiling fog. And the pain! It was as if he was being torn in two, as if the game had penetrated him and was ripping his flesh as he came out of it.

'What's wrong, Phoenix? You look terrible.'

Phoenix finally focused on Dad's anxious face. He was about to tell him about the pain, but something stopped him. The game had got under his skin, and no matter how much it had hurt he had to play again. He'd been home, he'd felt the promise of his destiny.

'It's OK,' he panted, trying desperately to recover from the shock of the hand on his shoulder. 'You gave me a fright.'

'Seems more than a fright to me. You look awful.'

'Honestly, you took me by surprise, that's all.'

'Well, sorry if I gave you a start, Phoenix. There's a phone call for you.'

Reluctantly, Phoenix unfastened the score bracelet, peeled off the mask and started to wriggle out of the suit. There was sweat this time, the sour sweat of fear. And all for a phone call.

Phone call indeed! He'd almost forgotten the stone cottage in Brownleigh existed.

6

If numbers can groan, that's what they were doing as Phoenix went to get the phone. Dad decided to shut down. He knew all about teenagers' phone calls! As first one, then another of the multiples of three glowed on the screen, he wondered what they meant.

How dare you? the hidden voice was saying. *How dare you break off? You cannot walk away from the game so easily. There's a whole world waiting to play. You will have to learn respect, young warrior. You will have to learn to stand in awe of the game. It is part of you now, just as it is part of me. I felt it too when you broke free. There's a connection, something I haven't felt for so long. You were meant to play. Enjoy it while you can, boy-fighter. Soon, it will penetrate the soft underbelly of your undeserving world. There will be no peace for the innocent. You must play this game to the end. To the bitter end.*

7

Phoenix awoke the next morning to the sound of the breeze snapping the curtains. He felt desperately tired and his head was pounding. It was as though something was probing his mind, draining him of life. He was experiencing a deep, numbing exhaustion. What had the game done to him? It was a quarter of an hour before he was able to swing his legs painfully out of bed and make his way to the bathroom. Washing and brushing his teeth made him feel a little better and he could finally think.

'Of course, it's Saturday.'

The thought started to loosen the hold of his headache.

'Yes, I can play all day if I want to.'

He remembered how angry he'd been with Laura for dragging him off it with an uneventful phone call the previous evening. This time he was going to declare himself out of bounds for the whole day. Nobody, but nobody was getting him off the computer until he was good and ready.

'Morning,' he called to Mum as he made his way downstairs. 'Is Dad in the study?'

'Whoa, whoa,' said Mum, emerging from the kitchen in her towelling dressing gown, a cup and tea towel in hand. 'What's the big rush?'

'The game,' Phoenix replied, following her into the kitchen. 'I'm going to get some breakfast and play.'

'I think you might be in for a bit of a disappointment,' said Mum, taking a sip of coffee. 'Your dad went out about half an hour ago, taking that suit thing with him.'

'He's what?'

'He packed all that game stuff away and chucked it in the car. He must have been working until well after midnight, because I went up to bed at half past eleven. Don't ask me what he's up to. He went back to the game after you turned in, and he didn't say a word to me this morning.'

Suddenly, there was a huge aching space where all of Phoenix's expectations for the day had been.

'But Pan had only just introduced me to the game.'

Mum reacted as if she had suffered an electric shock. She seemed to mouth the word *Pan*. The mug she had been drying fell and smashed on the floor.

'Look at that!' she cried, running her finger under the tap. 'Now I've cut myself.'

Phoenix stared in disbelief. What a reaction.

'I'm sick of hearing about that game,' snapped Mum. 'I wish John had never started it.'

Phoenix gave her time to calm down.

'Did he say where he was going?' he ventured after a few minutes.

'You've got to be joking,' said Mum. 'He didn't even have breakfast with me. That father of yours, he's getting worse.'

'And he's taken the lot?'

Phoenix couldn't believe it. The one day he would have had the time to really get into the game. Him, the guinea pig. And Dad had gone off with all the gear!

'What am I supposed to do all day?'

Mum smiled.

'What you did before you had the game, I suppose. Read, go swimming, call on your friends—'

'This isn't London,' Phoenix objected. 'I've only got one friend here.'

'Call on *her* then.'

'I'd rather play *The Legendeer*.'

That look came into Mum's face, the one she'd worn when she dropped the mug. It was a moment or two before she managed a reply.

'Oh, stop moaning,' she said. 'It's only a stupid game.'

38

Phoenix turned away. Stupid? Nobody who'd played it would say that.

The rain had stopped by the time he reached the High Street. He'd waited all of three hours before giving up on Dad. There was no sign of him and he hadn't phoned. It was after Phoenix's third minor tiff with Mum that he decided to call on Laura. The sun came out, garish and dazzling on the damp streets. The heat only added to his bad mood. He had a heat rash spreading across his chest. He felt itchy and uncomfortable and a headache was lurking. He reflected on a lousy morning. Not only was he locked out of the study and unable to play the game, he'd also made an unwelcome discovery in the shed. The back tyre of his bike was flat and there was no puncture kit.

'Looks like I'm walking to Laura's.'

Or maybe he was running. He caught sight of Steve Adams and his mates making their way past the Post Office. Perhaps they hadn't seen him.

'Hey, surprise, surprise, if it isn't Free Knickers.'

So much for wishful thinking.

'Get him!'

There were five of them, and they were coming at a run. They fancied the odds and Phoenix didn't. Not this time. He remembered Laura's warning. Steve carried a knife.

'You've had it this time, Free Knickers.'

Phoenix looked hopefully at the pelican crossing. The news wasn't good.

Wait, it told him.

Adams was patting his jacket.

'You haven't got it yet, have you? You're not wanted here.'

A bluff, Phoenix hoped, but he wasn't about to call it. For once, it wasn't fear that drove him, it was something he'd felt in the labyrinth – the shame of being beaten.

'You stay right there,' Adams ordered.

Phoenix fixed his enemy with a stare. Ten yards and closing. He glanced at the crossing. Still on *Wait*. The Saturday morning traffic was more dangerous than Adams, but he threw himself into the road nevertheless. He couldn't give Adams the satisfaction of beating him.

Behind him he heard warning shouts and a cry of horror: 'The boy's crazy.' '. . . He's going to get himself killed.'

He was dodging and weaving, holding up his hand to the startled and angry drivers. He heard the squeal of brakes. A near miss. But nothing was going to stop him now. Struggling to the middle of the road, he took a gulp of fume-filled air and weaved his way to the far pavement. He'd made it, but only thanks to an emergency stop by a private hire taxi.

'You young idiot!'

'Need their heads looking at, these kids.'

But Phoenix wasn't hanging around to listen. He had to put some distance between himself and Adams' gang.

Without so much as a backwards glance he ran off, cut through the alleyway between the bank and the church and scrambled down the embankment on the disused railway line. A quick sprint across the biscuit factory car park and he was at the corner of Laura's street. The gang wasn't following. But he was out of luck at Laura's too. Nobody was in.

'Wonderful,' he groaned, 'Absolutely rotten wonderful!'

He was just turning back into the High Street, glancing nervously from right to left for some sign of Adams, when he heard a car horn. It was Dad.

'You're back then,' Phoenix said, sliding into the passenger seat. Much as he resented Dad's disappearing act, he kept quiet about it. He didn't want to jeopardize his chance of playing the game again.

Dad checked the mirror and glanced over his shoulder before pulling out into the traffic.

'Mmm.'

His voice sounded flat.

'Something up?'

'You could say that.'

Phoenix felt a twinge of unease.

'Has this got something to do with the game?'

40

Dad nodded and pulled up at the traffic lights which had just turned to red.

'I had to send the suit back this morning.'

'You did what! Why?'

Dad rolled up his shirt sleeve to reveal a long scratch on his upper arm. It looked raised and angry.

'How did you get that?'

The lights changed to green.

'That's what I'd like to know. One minute I was playing the game, the next there was this burning sensation right down my arm.'

Phoenix started, remembering the charge of pain that had run through his own body. He still hadn't mentioned it.

When the lights changed, Dad drove over the bridge and turned left towards home.

'But I didn't notice anything sharp.'

'Me neither. But something caused this. One thing's for sure, you're not going to use that game until I've got some assurances about its safety.'

Phoenix stood on the pavement while Dad locked and alarmed the car. His frustration boiled over. 'Typical,' he snorted. 'You get a bit of a scratch and you send the whole thing back. Haven't you got any bottle?'

'Look,' Dad replied, struggling to contain his temper. 'All the accessories are made of the same material. I'm not taking any chances.'

'No, you never do.'

'Now that's enough!'

Phoenix looked at the cut. He hardly cared about the danger. There was something in the game, something hidden and exciting. Playing was all that mattered.

'You spoil everything! First you drag us all the way out here to live, then you ruin the only good thing that's happened to me.'

Phoenix didn't like the sound of his own voice, there was a cruelty he didn't intend, but he was furious with Dad. The game was gone, a game that had started to become part of him.

Still fighting to keep a lid on his temper, Dad turned his key in the front door. There was a note from Mum on the hall table.

Gone shopping. Back in an hour.

Dad ran his eyes over the yellow Post-It, then turned to face Phoenix. 'There's something I haven't told you.'

'I can't wait.'

'Just listen to me, will you?'

Phoenix grimaced. He knew he was being horrible, but he couldn't help it.

'OK, I'm listening.'

'I'd got as far as Theseus' journey through the badlands on the way to Athens. You know where I mean?'

'Yes, where he has to fight the bandits.'

'That's it. Anyway, I had no problem with most of the bad guys. I got past Periphetes, the cudgel man, and Sinis who tried to tie me to a couple of trees to rip me in half. I was having quite a good time, wasting them. I was really clocking up the points – a superhero. Then it started to get . . . weird.'

Phoenix was intrigued, so intrigued he forgot he was meant to be angry.

'How do you mean, weird?'

'Well, at first it was just fun. You know, baddy jumps up, hero kills baddy. The mother of all battles is fun when you know nobody gets hurt. Then I came to this castle. An old man invited me in. He was called—'

'Procrustes. Yes, I know the story.'

'Then you'll know he has this cute habit of tying people to a magic bed.'

'That's right. If you're too short for it, he stretches your limbs. If you're too tall, he—'

'Yes, he cuts off your feet. Well, I wish I'd known about old Procrustes—'

'But you must have known,' Phoenix interrupted. 'You do the story lines.'

'That's what I thought,' said Dad. 'But it appears there's more than one of us working on the plot, even on my levels.

I'm not like you and your mother. I skim the legends and pick the exciting bits, the stuff that will make good computer episodes. I'd never even heard of Procrustes and his magic bed. Anyway, you know the way you can touch and smell things in the game, well it turns out you can eat and drink as well.'

'You're kidding!'

'Oh, believe me, you can,' Dad insisted. 'Every physical sensation seems to have been incorporated into it. I had quite a supper at Procrustes' castle, but the wine must have been drugged because I woke up being tied to the bed. And before you say it, yes, he was going to stretch me. Luckily, my hands were still free and I got loose. Then Procrustes came at me with a razor-sharp cleaver. That's when I felt the pain in my arm. But it's crazy, the game couldn't cut you.'

Phoenix wasn't so sure. He couldn't get the Minotaur out of his head. The yellow eyes, the bellow that shook walls, the blood-smeared skin. It's not that he'd wanted to run. He'd *had* to. Phoenix was starting to think the game had a life of its own. But he wasn't going to tell Dad that. He still wanted to play it again. Something else he had to do. It was time to placate the old man.

'Of course not,' he said reassuringly. 'It'll be a sharp thread in the suit, that's all.'

'Mmm,' Dad replied dubiously.

'I mean,' Phoenix said hurriedly. 'What else could it be?'

'That's just it,' Dad answered. 'I can't imagine. The only thing I know is that something was wrong with the suit and I'm not taking any risks. I've written to Reede, telling him what I think of his game.'

'You haven't!'

'Oh, I have. I told him I was quite worried about safety.'

Phoenix relaxed. *Quite* worried, was that all Dad could say? With a protest as weak as that, Reede would soon have him singing a different tune.

'I'm sure it'll soon be sorted out,' he said, anxious to play again.

'Maybe,' Dad murmured, gazing thoughtfully into the garden.

Phoenix smiled to himself. If he knew Dad, he was bound to do whatever Reede wanted. After all, Dad was no hero.

8

The family were in the living room the following morning when Dad sprang out of his chair and flew to the door.

'What's he doing now?' groaned Mum.

'Beats me,' Phoenix replied.

'Unbelievable,' came Dad's voice. 'Un-flipping-believable.'

Mum and Phoenix reached the hallway together.

'What is?'

He was kneeling on the floor, surrounded by polystyrene packing, rummaging in a cardboard box.

'This.'

He held up a new Parallel Reality suit. It was identical to the last one, only in red.

'That's funny,' said Mum. 'There's no parcel post on a Sunday. Did you catch who delivered it?'

'Not really,' Dad answered. 'All I saw was a van pulling up in front of the house. It was halfway down the road before I got to the door. And look at this, there are two suits this time.'

'Isn't there a letter or anything?'

'Not a dicky-bird. Just the parcel. Honestly, what sort of cock-eyed operation is this Glen Reede running?'

'A pretty efficient one, by the look of it,' said Mum. 'You've got to admit, it's impressive, getting the suit replaced in 24 hours.'

Dad didn't reply. Instead, he folded the suit and put it back in the box.

'I don't have to give him anything. Tomorrow morning, this package goes right back where it came from. I'm not so much

45

as touching that program until I get cast-iron assurances about the game's safety.'

'Well, good for you,' said Mum. 'You stick by your guns.'

'That,' Dad told her as he opened the study door and stowed the package inside, 'is exactly what I intend to do.'

But the resolution only lasted a few hours. Dad got the e-mail from Reede about Magna-com's new safety measures at three o'clock. He was back-tracking by four.

'Damaged in transit,' he explained to Phoenix. 'A fine wire thread had worked loose. Reede's had the suit fully-lined to prevent a repeat. See.'

He held out the suit, displaying the new lining, a layer of fabric as fine and soft as the original.

'And I've got a cast-iron guarantee that the fault will be eliminated before the game's launch date.'

'I can't believe we've got the new suits already,' said Phoenix. 'They don't hang about, do they?'

'Not a bit.'

Dad's worries about the suit were quickly forgotten in the excitement of having the replacements but he was particularly enthusiastic about a new development announced in the e-mail. Whatever it was, it seemed to have tipped the balance. Dad was back on board.

'So do I get to have another go?' Phoenix asked eagerly. 'I *am* your guinea pig.'

'We both have another go,' said Dad, 'now there are two suits. I'm leaving nothing to chance this time. Wherever you go, whatever you do, I'll be right behind, shadowing you. The moment anything goes even slightly iffy, we're getting out.'

Phoenix thought it was an odd thing to say – *wherever you go*. After all, they would be right here in the study. Dad had made the point often enough himself; the sense of movement was an illusion.

'Could we just skip straight to the labyrinth? I want another crack at the Minotaur.'

'You're sure you want to?'

Phoenix nodded. Grateful for Glen Reede's e-mail, he slipped into the suit. And slipped was exactly the right word. There was hardly any friction at all.

Like a second skin.

'But before we start,' said Dad. 'Take a look at this. It's the next stage in developing the ultimate game, and it'll blow you away.'

He handed Phoenix a questionnaire.

'Go on, read it.'

'What, now?'

He was itching to get at the Minotaur.

'Yes, now. You won't be disappointed.'

'But what's it about?'

Dad smiled. 'Another innovation from the fertile mind of Glen Reede. You won't believe what he's come up with this time. He's not satisfied with the game as it stands. Now he's planning one that can be tailor-made to each individual player.'

'Never!'

Dad nodded.

'Imagine it. You send off a list of what – and who – you would have in your perfect game, and Magna-com will design it for you. I've never seen anything like this outfit. The ideas just flood out, and the technology is changing by the day. Astonishing.'

Intrigued, Phoenix started to fill it in straightaway.

'Look at this,' he said. 'A game for several players. You have to name your heroine and your villain.'

'Any candidates?' asked Dad.

Phoenix grinned. 'Oh yes.'

For heroine, he wrote *Laura Osibona*.

For villain, without any hesitation, he wrote *Steve Adams*.

For incidental characters, he jokingly added *John Graves*.

Completing the last question, about the cheats you wanted programmed into your game, Phoenix handed the form to Dad.

'Go on,' he said excitedly. 'Load the disc.'

Dad frowned.

'What did your last servant die of?'

'Boredom,' Phoenix quipped. 'Some idiot sent him to live in Brownleigh. Now can we get on with the game?'

Dad loaded the disc.

'Don't forget to skip forward.'

Dad nodded.

'The labyrinth awaits.'

9

It was dark in the palace of King Minos and it took Phoenix a few moments to get accustomed to the gloom.

'You there, Dad?' he whispered.

'Right behind you.'

They were edging cautiously down a flight of stone stairs.

'I thought we were starting at the labyrinth,' Phoenix hissed.

'We are. These are the steps leading down to the entrance. I should know. I helped design them.'

'And that light?'

Phoenix was pointing at a faint glimmer below them.

'Princess Ariadne,' said Dad. 'She's waiting with the ball of thread and the sword.'

'That's OK,' Phoenix told him impatiently. 'You don't need to tell me everything. I only wanted to know *where* I was. I know the legend better than you, remember.'

It was brighter at the bottom of the stairs. Torches stood in iron brackets, flaring with every whisper of breeze. In their flickering light he saw the dark-eyed girl who had watched him break and run. It was hard to believe she was no more than a graphic projection.

'Prince Theseus,' said Ariadne, approaching him. 'I was only able to slip away for a few minutes. My father is suspicious. Here.' She handed him the thread and sword. He felt the usual vibration against his wrist as his score built up. 'Take these. The thread will lead you back to the entrance. The sword—'

'Yes,' said Phoenix. 'I think I know what to do with the sword.'

When she saw Dad emerging from the blackness of the stairwell, Ariadne shrank back.

'Who's this?'

'This? Oh, he's my servant.'

Ariadne continued to dart suspicious glances at Dad. Reluctantly accepting his presence, she rested a hand on Phoenix's arm.

'May the gods go with you. Strike hard and strike well. Make the beast's death agony short. You must remember who he is.'

As Ariadne unlocked the door, Phoenix noticed Dad frowning.

'What?'

Dad shook his head.

Phoenix knew what he meant. *Not in front of the girl*. He waited until the door slammed shut before asking his question.

'Go on, Dad. What was that about? Something's bothering you.'

'It's what Ariadne said. She wanted you to kill the Minotaur quickly.'

'That's right. Don't tell me you've forgotten the legend, it's her half-brother.'

'Exactly,' said Dad. 'But I took that bit of the legend out. I thought it was too complicated for a computer game. I've been trying to keep it simple. I just wanted to cut straight to the action. Boy fights Monster, that'll do most kids.'

The Minotaur for one also wanted to cut to the action. No sooner were the words out of Dad's mouth than the beast was roaring menacingly in the dark depths of the maze.

'What's the big deal?' asked Phoenix. 'So somebody has added a few extra bits.'

'But this isn't *my* game. Phoenix, I'm calling this. Something's wrong.'

For a few moments, Phoenix wavered. Then, driving his own doubts to the back of his mind, he pleaded with Dad.

'Oh, come on. Just a few more minutes, and if you're still not happy, we'll call *Game Over*. That was the agreement.'

Dad looked doubtful, but finally nodded. Phoenix felt like

changing his mind a few seconds later. The beast was close, snorting and panting in the tunnels. Then it bellowed, a sound so loud and harsh that it buried itself deep into his brain.

'Give me the sword,' said Dad.

He was definitely rattled.

'No way,' said Phoenix, displaying his score. 'It gave me fifty points. Here, you can have the thread.'

He was already fighting an uphill battle with his own fear. He didn't need Dad making things worse. Did he have to be so jumpy? Phoenix breathed deeply, trying to compose himself. He knew every line of the beast's face. At the thought of those yellow eyes, he felt a rush of terror.

Only a game, he repeated again and again in his mind, it's only a game.

But every little thing that had happened so far had drilled the fear deeper and deeper into his brain. When the door had slammed shut, it was like a coffin lid being screwed down. And Dad's concern about the re-writing of the game, for all Phoenix's brave words, was worrying.

'That smell!' gasped Dad. 'I can hardly breathe.'

Phoenix knew what it was. It was the rank odour of rotting flesh. Maybe Magna-com were laying the special effects on a bit thick. It was stifling.

'Are you all right?'

He looked pasty.

'Not really.'

'Come on. Just a bit longer.

They were creeping forward, Phoenix crouching sword in hand, Dad playing out the thread. On they went into endless passageways, turning first to the left, then to the right, and never quite knowing the shifting whereabouts of the beast.

'I can hear it moving,' Dad whispered. 'It's behind us.'

Phoenix could hear the beast. It bellowed again, like a great ox, shaking the mortar between the stone blocks of the dungeon walls. Dust fell like fine, dry rain. Just like the first time.

'Listen!'

It was the unmistakable scrape of giant hooves on the stone floor. A moment later a dark muzzle appeared. Yellow eyes blazed through the darkness, vivid under the heavy brows.

'It's here. Phoenix, get ready, it's here.'

Phoenix could feel the hilt of the sword sliding in his clammy grasp. He was feeling the same urge to flee as he had the other times, but he had to overcome it.

Had to.

Come on, just do it. Make your move.

But the beast held its ground, targeting its victims with a long, cold, unwavering stare. The predator's stare.

'We can stop the game,' Dad murmured.

Are you sure about that, thought Phoenix, remembering the blinding pain last time.

'Give me a little bit longer,' said Phoenix. 'I can win. I'll do it this time.'

Then something flashed.

'It's armed.'

Phoenix watched in horror as the huge, sinewy arms swung a heavy, metal-studded club.

'That's not right,' Dad exclaimed. 'I didn't give it any weapons. It's got enough advantages already. I'm calling it, Phoenix. Somebody's been tinkering with the game. It's fixed.'

'Don't say that,' gulped Phoenix.

The beast stepped forward raising the club to shoulder-height, its upper arms bunching massively. Phoenix glanced at the score on his bracelet. Eighty points. He was going to defend them with his life.

'Come on then,' he said, gritting his teeth. 'This time I'm not running.'

With an ear-splitting roar, the beast swung its club shattering the sword into a dozen fragments. Phoenix stared in disbelief at his grazed palm and the shards of metal bouncing on the floor of the labyrinth. Then he turned his attention to the hideous face looming above him. His score was in free fall. The attack was wiping out his precious points.

'That's it,' yelled Dad. 'This time I'm definitely calling it. *Game over!*'

Seconds later, Phoenix and Dad were ripping at their masks, panicking a little when they took so long to give.

'I can't get it off,' cried Dad.

'I know.'

'You mean this has happened to you before?' Dad demanded, finally tugging it free.

Phoenix kept quiet about the pain he had felt, but he admitted the difficulty removing the mask. 'Yes, it has. When Laura phoned.'

'For goodness' sake. You've *got* to tell me when anything like this happens.'

'What, so you can stop me playing?'

'If that's what it takes to make the game safe, yes.'

Phoenix rolled his eyes.

'Typical.'

Dad chose to ignore the comment. 'That's another fault to report,' he grumbled, wincing slightly as he pulled his hand from the suit. 'Why on Earth didn't you tell me?'

Because I've got to play.

When they were finally free of the suits, they stood panting. Before they could exchange a word, Mum was at the door, anxiety etched on her face.

'What's happened?'

'It's nothing,' panted Phoenix. 'Just the game.'

'A game that's been interfered with,' said Dad. 'Something is very odd and I'm going to find out what.'

Phoenix said nothing. Infuriating as Dad could be, he was right about one thing. This was no ordinary game.

10

'I'm your what!' Laura clearly didn't know how to take the news. 'I'm your heroine?'

'That's right,' said Phoenix. 'I can't wait to see how this pegs out. I don't understand how you and Adams—'

'Hang on. What's Steve Adams got to do with anything?'

'Well, when I wrote down your name as the heroine, I gave Adams as the villain. But like I say, I don't see how it can work. I mean, if they're going to program people into these personalized games, they'll need a photo or something at least. Unless they start grabbing the real people themselves.'

Despite the slight headache he had been nursing ever since he got up, Phoenix smiled. That's the sort of thing Dad might be expecting. The mood he was in, he wouldn't even put kidnapping past Magna-com. It was incredible how seriously he was taking this game. He wasn't really to blame, though. *The Legendeer* was addictive all right. It made him feel more alive than he'd ever been. If pain couldn't keep him away, what could?

'Are you sure this is for real?' asked Laura. 'You're not making it up?'

'Of course I'm not making it up! What do you take me for?'

'Well,' said Laura, 'you did tell the whole class stories were better than life.'

'Yes, but that's—'

He looked around the people on the packed bus and realized that not one of them would be worrying about myths and monsters. It wasn't the sort of thing people thought about on a

54

Monday morning on their way to school or work.

'All I can say is, Dad is working on a game and it's as fantastic as I've told you. More so.'

Laura gave him a sceptical look. 'I never know how to take you.'

'Laura,' said Phoenix. 'There's one thing you should know about me. I *never* lie.'

He said it in all seriousness, so Laura's reaction was all the more shocking. She laughed. No, that's not quite the word for it. She gave a shrill whinny of a laugh that had half the bus staring at her.

'Sorry, Phoenix, but everybody lies.'

He stuck to his guns.

'I don't.'

'Then you must be some sort of saint.'

Not a saint, just somebody with a destiny.

'I'm telling you,' he insisted. 'Magna-com does exist, and Dad is involved in developing a personalized game.'

'So, you're telling me you can put me in your game?'

'Yes. And sometime soon they'll be able to customize you a game of your own.'

'OK, *The Wizard of Oz*, it's my favourite film. You could make something of that. I'll be Dorothy. You can be the lion looking for his courage.'

Phoenix frowned. He had enough with his headache without Laura winding him up.

'Now you're just being silly.'

'Oh, am I? Well, you just look at it from where I'm sitting. You tell me about this amazing game, but you won't let me play it.'

'I explained that,' Phoenix said. 'Dad would kill me if he knew I'd even told you about it.'

'Let's change the subject, eh?' said Laura. 'I don't want to quarrel with you. You're my best friend.'

Phoenix seized eagerly on her words.

'Am I?'

'You know you are.'

Phoenix wanted to hear more, but he'd reckoned without Steve Adams.

'Well, well,' he said. 'If it isn't the lovely Laura. And, oh dear, what bad taste you've got. What can you be doing with this deadbeat?'

'Oh, leave off, Steve,' said Laura. 'Don't you think this has gone far enough?'

'Oh no,' said Adams, the smile instantly leaving his face. 'I haven't even started. I'll have you, Free Knickers.'

Aware of Laura watching him, Phoenix decided to play it cool. 'Adams,' he said matter-of-factly. 'I'll choose my own friends, thank you very much.'

'You'll do as you're told,' said Adams. 'You think you're so clever, don't you, swanning in here like you own the place. Well, I'm going to show you exactly who runs Brownleigh. I'll be waiting for you tonight. And just to make sure you don't try to do a runner, I'm going to spread the word all round school. You and me on the wasteground opposite the gates. Don't even think about bottling out, or you'll never be able to hold your head up round here again. See you, Free Knickers.'

As Phoenix watched Adams making his way back down the bus, Laura caught his attention.

'Take no notice,' she said. 'He's all talk.'

'You sure about that?'

'Oh Phoenix! You're not going to do it? You're not going to fight him?'

Phoenix was struggling with the discomfort behind his eyes. 'It doesn't look like he's giving me much choice.'

Laura sighed.

'Well, I am. You walk away. Nobody will blame you. Steve Adams is a thug. Just give him a wide berth.'

'Oh, I will,' said Phoenix. 'If he lets me.'

Adams had no intention of letting Phoenix off the hook. All day long Adams' cronies were sidling up to him, reminding him that he was expected on the wasteground at 3.15. For once, Adams took a back seat in the continual goading.

'Don't let it get to you,' Laura told him during the lunch hour. 'You don't look quite right, you know.'

Phoenix was tempted to tell her it wasn't because of Adams. The headache he'd woken up with had turned into a general feverishness. His skin prickled and his eyes felt as if they were being pushed back into their sockets. Something told him this might have something to do with the game too. Even when he was little, the attacks had never been this frequent.

'It'll be OK.'

But the headache didn't let up, nor did the campaign. It continued throughout the afternoon with notes passed across the classroom.

'Ignore it,' Laura advised between lessons.

But by home time, Phoenix knew it would take a miracle to prevent the fight.

'Just walk away,' Laura pleaded as they headed for the school gates.

Phoenix smiled thinly. Because of the headache, he didn't feel like speaking, or even nodding his head. But ahead of him was a reception party of Adams' mates. A buzz of excitement was running through the crowds of schoolkids jostling past them. Everybody knew about the fight.

'Keep walking,' said Laura. 'I've told you before. He carries a weapon.'

But by the time he reached Adams' cronies, he knew there was no avoiding the fight.

'He's waiting for you,' they taunted.

Phoenix didn't even give them a glance.

'You're coming with us,' they announced, surrounding him.

The headache was a searing band of pain behind his eyes. He no longer had the strength or the will to resist. As he accompanied them across the road, he realized that Laura had disappeared.

'Surprise, surprise,' crowed Adams. 'Look who's here.'

'There's no need to do this,' said Phoenix feebly, struggling with the drumbeat in his head.

He tried to break out of the circle of onlookers, but they shoved him back in.

'Oh yes,' said Adams, rushing him, 'there is.'

Phoenix took the full force of the charge on his right side and was spun round. The world turned, sickening him to the core. He lost his footing and fell. As he hit the ground, for a split second he saw something. Not stars, but numbers. The numbers from the monitor screen.

What's happening to me?

It was as if the game was reaching out, calling him back.

For a moment, he was between two worlds.

Adams took immediate advantage, getting behind his opponent and pinning his arms. Phoenix struggled, but Adams had a powerful grip. Wriggling one arm loose, Phoenix prised Adams' hands off. The respite didn't last long. As Phoenix turned to face his opponent, Adams sprang at him, the force of the attack pinning him to the ground.

'You're going to regret ever coming to Brownleigh,' Adams snarled.

That was almost funny. Phoenix had been regretting it for months. Sitting astride Phoenix, Adams steadied himself, but Phoenix forced a hand under the other boy's jaw shoving back his head. He could feel Adams shifting backwards. The move soon had him half unseated, grunting with discomfort.

But Adams wasn't done yet. He crouched over Phoenix, punching hard.

'Get him, Steve!'

'Batter him!'

Phoenix's head was pounding. The oppressive heat was overpowering. Even worse was the smell – the choking animal musk of the labyrinth.

I'm going mad.

'Don't let him off, Steve!'

'Get into him!'

Phoenix was shocked by the savage beating he was taking, but he wasn't about to give up. He had more pride than that.

'Get off me!' He spat, blood dripping from his nose.

But Adams was in command. He twisted his fingers round Phoenix's tie and punched down into his face. That's when Phoenix started to retch.

'Look out Steve, he's gagging.'

Adams drew away. A moment later, Phoenix was suddenly, violently sick.

'Ugh, the disgusting pig!'

Phoenix was leaning to one side, coughing and spluttering. Once Adams had released him, he wiped his face and rolled over, feeling drained. He was looking up at the sky. Adams had gone. All Phoenix could hear were the retreating footfalls of the gang. As he rose unsteadily to his feet, he noticed Laura hurrying through the school gates in the company of two of the teachers. But he didn't wait for them. He didn't want to share his humiliation with anyone else. From somewhere he found the strength to run. He was in no mood to talk. He wanted to lick his wounds.

Alone.

11

Dad was the only one in when he got home.

'What happened to you?' he asked. 'No, don't tell me. It's that lad isn't it? What's his name?'

'Adams. You're not going to tell Mum, are you?'

'I think she ought to know, don't you?'

'She'll be straight down to school if she knows. She'll make things worse.'

'I don't see how. Look at the state of you.'

Phoenix continued to plead his case. 'She'll make a show of me.'

'That's daft talk.'

'What do you know?'

'I was your age once, you know.'

Phoenix sneered. 'Yeah sure, I bet you never had to put up with anything like this. Look, Dad, I just want to fight my own battles.'

'Not doing too well though, are you?'

'I'll be fine. Just don't blow me up. I'll never forgive you if you do.'

'You know what?' Dad said, his eyes flashing with hurt. 'Sometimes you and your mother treat me worse than the dirt on your shoes. What do I do that's so wrong?'

It was a good question, and one for which Phoenix didn't have an answer. He regretted his outburst.

'Sorry. I just want to sort it my own way. Give me a chance. Please.'

Dad examined Phoenix's face.

'Should be able to patch you up,' he said. 'Yes, you'll get

60

away with it. There'll be one or two bruises to explain away, so you'd better get your thinking cap on. A good excuse, mind. Something convincing.'

'So, you're not going to tell her? Thanks Dad.'

'No,' said Dad, 'I won't tell her. Despite what you think of me, I do understand. I've been there myself.'

Phoenix looked at him. He couldn't see it somehow.

'There is one condition though.'

'What's that?'

'You've got until the end of the week to sort things out with this Adams lad, or it will be me knocking on the Headteacher's door. Got that?'

'Yes Dad, got it.'

By the time Mum got in from her meeting, Dad and Phoenix were in the study. They'd sunk their differences enough to tackle *The Legendeer* together. Mum had to be satisfied with a grunted hello from behind the closed door. Once she had accepted that they were in for the duration, they put on their suits and descended into the labyrinth again.

'I'm going to win this time,' said Phoenix as they walked down the stone steps of King Minos' palace to meet Ariadne.

'Sure,' said Dad, 'you're going to win.'

But there was an unease in his voice. He couldn't forget what had happened last time.

Phoenix led the way to the bottom. It was the same as the day before. The torches flared, the dark-eyed girl approached them. He felt a rush of excitement – the game was underway. But the moment she started speaking, Phoenix too was reminded of the last time they had played.

Ariadne had departed completely from her usual text.

'You have to flee,' she said urgently, her normally sing-song voice little more than a strangled croak. 'Both of you. Get out of here. It's not what you think.'

'What do you mean?' asked Dad.

Ariadne glanced around furtively. 'I can't talk,' she said. 'King Minos' spies are everywhere.'

Phoenix found this disquieting. A note of imbalance had entered the game. Something wasn't right. Ariadne had said King Minos, and not *my father*. Very strange.

'But one thing I can tell you,' Ariadne concluded. 'This place is evil.'

Unease pinched the hairs on the back of Phoenix's neck.

'What are you up to?' he demanded. 'Is this a trick?'

Judging by the look on Dad's face, he was already having second thoughts. Phoenix had to act. The game was everything he had always wanted, something big, something extreme. Something to tell him he wasn't the sort of kid to get pushed around by the likes of Adams. Then he saw his chance. Just as Ariadne was about to speak again, the words seemed to strangle in her throat. She was holding the side of her neck as if she was in pain. That's when Phoenix remembered. The key to the labyrinth was where it always was, hanging from Ariadne's necklace.

'Come on, Dad. We're going in.'

Snatching the key from the gasping Ariadne, he turned the lock and plunged into the labyrinth. The score on his bracelet had already reached ninety. The best yet. Once inside the tunnel, he started creeping forward. It wasn't long before the beast's roar filled the maze.

'Roar yourself hoarse if you want,' said Phoenix. 'This time, I'm going to finish the job.'

As if encouraging him, the points display clicked on for no apparent reason, reaching the magic hundred. He'd scored three figures for the first time.

He reached the meeting of the ways and paused. He was still wondering which way to go when he felt hot breath on his neck. He cried out in spite of himself.

'No!'

But it was Dad.

'Don't creep up on me like that. That's the second time you've scared the life out of me.'

Dad was in no **mood** to apologize. His eyes were bulging and a vein was throbbing in his temple. He was beside himself.

'You young idiot!' he bawled. 'Pull a trick like that again and I'll ground you for a month. I thought I told you we weren't going into the labyrinth. Don't you think it's a bit funny when even the game's characters start warning you off? That poor girl needed our help. I think she'd had some sort of seizure. Do you realize that I had to leave her to suffer just so I could come after you?'

'She's all right,' Phoenix retorted, suppressing his own doubts. 'That's all part of it. You're not going to let the game win, are you? Don't you recognize a con when you see one? Look, I've scored 100 already. I'm not giving up now.'

'Phoenix,' said Dad. 'I'm not arguing with you. We're getting out of here.'

'Bottle out if you want,' Phoenix replied angrily, determined to find the courage he'd lacked in the fight with Adams. 'I'm staying.'

Dad had obviously decided he wasn't going to waste another word on Phoenix, because he started manhandling him towards the door.

'You're coming with me.'

'No,' cried Phoenix, straining against his father's grip. 'No I'm not, and you can't make me.'

Dad dragged him closer to the door.

'Oh, can't I?'

That's when he loosened his hold.

'What the—'

The door had shut behind them.

'It's locked.'

He pounded on it.

'Ariadne, can you hear me? Let us out.'

There was female laughter, but it wasn't Ariadne's gentle tones they heard. There was a razor edge of cruelty in *this* woman's voice.

'Who is that?' Dad demanded. 'Who's there? Stop playing games. Let us out. Now!'

But the laughter continued, reverberating in the darkness.

'That does it,' said Dad. 'Game over.'

Only the game didn't end. Instead, the beast bellowed its blood lust from the heart of the maze.

'Game over!' Dad repeated.

But the labyrinth was in no mood to let go. Terror was closing round them like a claw.

'Game over! Game over!'

The beast's cry echoed through the labyrinth, an insane series of thunderclap animal howls.

'Phoenix,' Dad ordered. 'Take off your mask.'

His hands were already tugging at the skin around his chin.

'What is this?' he said, his voice betraying real fear. 'I can't feel the join. I can't feel the mask at all.'

Phoenix tried. He too was lurching over into skin-prickling panic.

'Me neither.'

They could hear the beast stamping through the tunnels, dragging its club behind it.

'This is wrong,' said Dad. 'Very wrong.'

Now even Phoenix was having second thoughts. Horror was pounding in his heart.

'You out there,' Dad cried, beating the door with his fists. 'Whoever you are. This is no joke. Let us out this minute.'

For a moment Phoenix glimpsed eyes looking back at them through the hatch in the door, but they weren't the soft, brown eyes of Ariadne. These eyes blazed, just like the beast's.

Somehow, they were made of the same primeval brutishness.

'We've got to run,' said Dad. 'If we stay here, it's got us cornered.'

Somewhere in the back of his mind, Phoenix knew this didn't make sense.

It can't hurt us. It's not real.

The terrible braying resumed, worse than ever.

It's a game, just a game.

But that single, common-sense thought was swallowed up by a tidal wave of terror. Fear coiled in the blackness then broke over them with unstoppable power.

'Phoenix! Move, this way.'

And they were running, running for their lives. He noticed the score on the bracelet. Eighty!

But how? Then he remembered.

'Dad! I've dropped the thread.'

He fell to his knees feeling for the string in the darkness. He hardly dared stretch out his fingers, for fear of brushing against the beast's gore-clogged hooves.

'Forget it,' said Dad. 'It can't help us now. Just run.'

They could hear the beast stamping somewhere close behind them.

'It's gaining on us. Run!'

They emerged into a large open space. It was hexagon-shaped. In the centre lay a filthy straw mattress. The heart of the labyrinth.

'Got to think,' said Dad. 'Come on, Phoenix, you like these games. What do you do when you're stuck?'

'Play a cheat, of course.'

'That's it,' said Dad. 'The cheats have been programmed in. But how do we use them?'

'You've got me,' said Phoenix. 'I mean, there's no keyboard. We're *in* the game.'

'That's it then,' said Dad. 'That means the cheats must be in it too. *Physically* in it.'

'Sounds good to me,' said Phoenix, his bravery crumbling as he clutched at straws. 'We've just got to find them.'

'Oh my!'

Dad's body was sagging against his, a heavy sack of despair. The beast had just appeared in the room.

'Dad,' Phoenix panted. 'You start looking. I'll try to keep him off you.'

For all the fear drumming inside him, Phoenix was still half convinced this was all some elaborate computer adventure. He could conquer the beast. And even if he lost, there was always another day.

Dad didn't share even a shred of Phoenix's hope. To face the beast was to die.

'Don't be so stupid—'

'I'm not,' Phoenix shouted. 'If you don't like my idea, try coming up with a better one.'

Dad hesitated, then reluctantly entered the nearest tunnel. Phoenix held the hilt of the sword tightly, and kept moving from side to side, skipping like an acrobat. He'd learned something from the last confrontation – don't take the beast on directly. He remembered the fragments of sword clattering on the floor.

If he could only avoid the murderous swing of the club, if he could just thrust under the Minotaur's defences. But the beast didn't give him time to think. It rushed him suddenly, flailing madly with the club. Masonry and dust flew in the gloom, pattering against the walls. Phoenix was overwhelmed. It was impossible to hold his ground under the frenzied onslaught.

'No, no-o!'

The score was down to seventy.

'Phoenix,' Dad called from the tunnel. 'What is it, what's wrong?'

The club whistled past his head. His score dropped to sixty.

'Dad. Help me.'

He could hear his father's footsteps in the tunnel behind him.

'Phoenix!'

The beast lunged again, smashing the sword from Phoenix's hands. He'd broken it like a toothpick.

The score was crashing. Fifty. Forty-five.

What am I doing? I'm a kid. I can't fight monsters.

Phoenix was hauling himself backwards, his feet lashing feebly at the oncoming beast.

Lowering its head, the Minotaur moved in for the kill.

'Dad!'

Then a surprisingly strong pair of hands was dragging him back. The deadly horns drilled into solid stone. With a shriek of rage, the beast twisted and tore at the floor. Mud, stone and foul water exploded around it.

'Run Phoenix,' cried Dad, relaxing his grip. 'Just run.'

Now they were flying, colliding with hidden walls and pillars in the blackness, but scrambling on, oblivious to the pain of a jarred shoulder or a bruised knee. And all the while the beast was coming, growling, snarling, roaring its hatred and its hunger.

'Dad,' Phoenix yelled suddenly. 'What's that?'

There was something in the wall. It was the size of a phone box, but in the shape of a kind of pyramid, a tetrahedron. It was silvery and distinct from the rest of the masonry and bore a bull's head symbol on the top. It was giving off an electronic buzz, the first reminder that this was, in fact, a game.

'That's it,' said Dad, hope rising for the first time in his reedy voice. 'It has to be. It's a terminal of some sort. It operates the cheat – the escape.'

The beast was at the end of the tunnel, dark and massive in the half-light. It seemed to hammer the air with its presence, shocking the breath out of its prospective victims.

'You first, son.'

Phoenix entered and felt a burst of energy around him.

'This is it,' he screamed, a cry that was half joy, half horror as the beast advanced.

'Then get through,' shouted Dad. 'And take my hand. When you get through, keep pulling. Whatever you do, don't let go.'

Phoenix hurled himself into the shimmering, yielding energy-burst, the gate between game and home.

'Don't let go!'

But the beast roared again, the rancid heat of its breath blasting into Phoenix's face. He screamed and threw himself through the gate – back into Dad's study.

To his horror, the room was empty. This time he and Dad hadn't been there at all, twitching in their PR suits. They had vanished bodily into the game.

Phoenix reached into the gate, but his fingers clawed at emptiness. He'd done it. He'd done the most terrible thing. He'd let go!

'Dad,' he shrieked, drowning in guilt. 'Dad!'

The gate was still shimmering, an oval of light in the study. It was still open. Phoenix thrust his hand into the light, reaching into the monstrous parallel world. Nothing. He stared at the computer screen. Dad was fleeing towards the gate. The beast was almost upon him. It was impossible to separate the two blurred figures.

'Dad!'

Then there was a dark shape in the gate. Dad? Or the beast? Phoenix fell back. Please, not that. In his panic, he almost pulled the plug from the wall. But Dad was still in there somewhere. He couldn't just abandon him. Then the shape took on recognizable form.

'Dad, thank goodness.'

'Phoenix,' Dad snapped. 'The suit, get it off. Now!'

As Phoenix peeled off the suit, Dad reached for the computer and switched off. The oval of light vanished. This time it really was game over.

He was running through the passageways again.

I have abandoned him, left him to his fate.

Behind him Phoenix could hear Dad's cries. The beast's bellows mixed with his screams.

It's tearing him apart and I have abandoned him.

Phoenix rested his forehead against the slimy stonework.

How could I?

I have to go back.

He retraced his steps through the gloomy tunnels, listening for a clue to the beast's whereabouts. But the maze was silent. He stumbled over something in the dark. Or somebody.

'Dad?'

He knelt down and examined the body, forcing himself to touch the bloodstained face.

It wasn't Dad.

Maybe I didn't betray you.

'Dad?'

He moved on, discovering four more of the beast's victims. He was seized by panic.

'Where are you?'

Then a shaft of light fell on his face. Dad was with Laura.

'You're alive.'

But they weren't looking at him. Their eyes were trained on a spot just behind him. He turned slowly. Two yellow eyes were staring at him. Hot, sickly breath was steaming from its nostrils. The beast! Phoenix watched in horror as its huge muscular arms curled round Dad and Laura, snapping ribs and grinding flesh.

'Phoenix,' they were screaming. 'Help us!'

He hung on to their arms but the beast was too strong.

'Don't let go. Please don't let go.'

But his courage failed. The beast vanished into the darkness with its fading victims.

'*No!*'

Phoenix sat bolt upright in bed. He was clammy with sweat and his head was pounding.

'What's happening to me?'

Moments later Dad came running into the room in his pyjamas.

'What is it? What's wrong?'

Phoenix felt stupid.

'It was a dream, Dad. I had a nightmare. Sorry if I woke you.'

The tension in Dad's face relaxed.

'Bad dreams, eh? I've been having a nightmare myself. I'm working through the game, then a terrible thought occurs to me. I'm not playing the game. *It's* playing *me*. I must be going crazy.'

'That goes for both of us.'

'Anyway, try to get some shuteye. It's been a wild day.'

Phoenix smiled.

'You can say that again.'

Dad walked to the door.

'Goodnight, son.'

But Phoenix didn't want to let him go without another attempt at an apology. Part of him was still playing the game. He could feel Dad's hand slipping from his grasp, his whole being filled with the agony of loss.

69

'Sorry I let you down. In the labyrinth, I mean.'

'Forget it.'

But it didn't sound like Dad had forgotten it. There was a curious hollowness about his voice, as if something had gone from him. Trust perhaps. Dad was about to close the door, when he paused.

'Forget the game too. You are not to go in the study. Do you understand that? Never.'

This time, there were no arguments. Just then, Phoenix didn't think either of them should chance playing again.

'Yes Dad, I understand.'

'I've had enough of this, Phoenix. That wasn't virtual reality. We were somewhere else.'

Phoenix nodded.

'Tomorrow morning I'm going to get to the bottom of all this. I'm going to find out exactly what Mr Glen Reede is playing at.'

'And if he won't tell you?'

'Then I'll find out for myself. I'll find out what's going on. Either that, or I'll destroy it.'

Even then, Phoenix couldn't shake the feeling that the game was part of him. He was the only one who could play and win.

'Dad, don't even try!'

'Why not? I've had it with Magna-com. I don't owe them anything. Anyway, I'm going to have one more go at understanding this game, then I'm telling Mr Glen Reede I'm finished with him.'

'You're resigning?'

'I'm thinking about it.'

Phoenix felt the weight of disappointment in his father's voice. The room filled with the distance between them. His voice shook as he answered, 'Goodnight, Dad.'

12

From the time of their return from the labyrinth, only Dad entered the study. He became a man obsessed. This thing was dangerous. He had to know just how dangerous. So John Graves set himself a task. He was going to crack the secret of the game, then he was going to destroy it. What's more, he knew that the numbers were a stepping stone. Crack their mysterious code and he would be on his way to thwarting Reede. So he alone stared at the encrypted message, he alone struggled with the numbers.

You'd like to read my thoughts, wouldn't you, John Graves? You'd like to pick my brains and then destroy me. I even had to remind poor Ariadne where her loyalties lie. That's right, suddenly it seems that my creatures would like to have a mind of their own. But the boy Phoenix has a feel for my world. No, more than a feel. That's right, our little Theseus has an instinct. Who knows, in time he could prove himself a worthy opponent. He is what I've been looking for, a believer, one I can use to test the game. The Legendeer is his destiny. He knows it, I know it. Why not? I can't unleash the game for a month. I've been waiting this long, I can afford to be patient. A little sport, then it will be time to get down to the real business. Coming soon, the bargain of the century. My world for yours.

John Graves continued to stare at the screen. Who knows, if he had understood even a little of the meaning of the procession of numbers, he might have worked with even greater urgency.

Phoenix tapped lightly on the door. 'Dad?'

'Can't talk now, son.' His voice was distant, as if he was speaking from another world entirely.

I didn't mean to betray you.

Why didn't I just hang on? Why did I have to let go?

'Are you working on the game? I—'

'Leave this to me, Phoenix.'

I can't leave it to you. I'm the one who plays the game.

'But Dad—'

Why wouldn't he listen? Suddenly, Phoenix didn't want to keep anything secret. Not the pain, not the sense of belonging. He had to stop Dad playing.

'But nothing, Phoenix. Leave me to sort it.'

So Phoenix walked on down the hall and dropped heavily on to the couch. Just like he had the night before and the night before that and the night before that. Except for a few snatched hours of sleep, Dad had hardly surfaced from his study since their last brush with the Minotaur. He'd said something strange once.

'I'm preparing a bomb for Glen Reede.'

After that, scarcely another word. He'd even started taking his meals in the study. Anything so that he could stay at the PC. Phoenix knew his father was getting himself deeper and deeper into something he didn't understand, and it scared him.

'I'd leave him to it,' Mum advised.

Phoenix groaned 'But how can I? I'm meant to be with him. It's my game as much as his. More. Dad doesn't know what he's dealing with.'

'Would you care to explain that?'

Frankly, thought Phoenix, I wouldn't. Somehow, the game gave him a sense of himself, of what he might be. It scared him all right, but he still felt he could beat it. He could be a hero. Not Dad though. He was an outsider.

'I'm still listening,' Mum said.

In some ways, she was the strongest of the three of them. She was quiet and modest, but her dark eyes saw right through her husband and son, and once she had made up her mind, she rarely changed it. Quietly, and without making a fuss, she held the family together even when the strains were as obvious as at present. Now that she sensed something was wrong, she

72

wanted Phoenix to explain himself. He knew he had no choice.

'It's the feeling I get when I'm playing,' Phoenix told her. 'I belong there. I'm . . . I'm *home*. But how can I feel at home in hell? I must sound really stupid.'

'No, not really,' said Mum. 'It's our game. We all had a part in creating it, remember.'

'Not as much as we thought,' said Phoenix.

'I know what you mean,' Mum said. 'But you've got the same feeling I had when I was writing the script for your father. It wasn't so much that I was telling the stories. They were telling themselves *through* me.'

Phoenix met her look.

'That's it Mum, that's exactly it. We're part of this.'

He twitched open the curtains and stared outside where the trees were threshing in the strong night wind. Mum was a good listener and talking to her seemed to make everything clear. He told her about his forays into the game and the growing feeling that it was bigger than he was. She didn't say a word, but from time to time her eyes widened, especially when he mentioned the god of mischief, Pan.

'Hang on,' he said, as if thinking straight for the first time. 'What was it you said before?'

'About what exactly?'

'I know. You said it was *our* game, but it isn't. We've been fooling ourselves. Maybe we feel we're part of it, but I don't think we created the game at all. I don't think we created *any* of it. We retold a few of the legends, Dad played with the elements of the game, but we didn't do anything new. It was all there for us, ready-made.'

Mum gave him a questioning look.

'It seems so obvious now,' Phoenix continued. 'Sure, when we picked the Greek myths we thought it was our choice. But they were there at the top of the options, along with the vampires and all the other legends. We were bound to choose them. Do you remember what Dad said?'

Mum shook her head slowly.

'He said he was only a scene-shifter. Somebody else made the jigsaw. All he did was move the pieces around.'

By then, Phoenix might have expected Mum to be questioning his sanity but, instead, she was listening intently.

'Go on.'

Encouraged, Phoenix let the ideas spill out. All the things he'd half felt or half thought. *The Legendeer* was more than a matter of graphics and a story line. It always had been. It was a living thing, a thing with power and a life independent of the PC. The machine was a vehicle for the game, the sheath for its chrysalis stage, and that's all. *The Legendeer* was somehow both primitive and all knowing. It was able to reach out. It could twist time and space. It played the player.

'That's right,' Phoenix exclaimed. 'It's been playing us.'

Dad had mentioned it more than once, the way the game was constantly changing, evolving, the way bits were being added without his knowing it. It was obvious.

'The game's alive!'

The thought filled Phoenix with horror. He had been at war with himself for days. Part of him, the instinctive part, wanted to play, to fulfil his destiny. But the greater part of him was taking control. All he wanted was to take a hammer and smash the computer so nobody could ever play it again, so that nobody could ever put themselves in danger.

'Dad!' cried Phoenix. 'We've got to get him off that computer.'

Mum wasn't arguing. They hurried down the hall.

'John, talk to me,' said Mum. 'I'm worried about you.'

'Worried?' Dad repeated. 'No need to worry about me. I'm a big boy now.'

He turned the lock and opened the door slowly, until he was peering out at them.

'Look Dad,' said Phoenix, going for broke, 'I think the game's alive. It thinks. It does things. It could even be dangerous.'

Dad smiled grimly.

'Only just worked that out, have you?'

'So you know!' cried Mum.

'Oh, I know all right. I knew before either of you did.' He unlocked the door and looked at them. His eyes were hard, staring. 'Shall I tell you what I know? There is no Magna-com. There's no office, no factory, no nothing. Just a website and a bank account that pays me each month by computerized credit transfer.'

Mum reacted first.

'But I don't understand.'

'Well,' Dad confessed, 'that makes three of us. It's true enough. There isn't even a Glen Reede. Want to know what Glen Reede is? It's an anagram, a stupid kid's anagram.'

He handed Phoenix a sheet of paper.

The letters GLEN REEDE were rearranged to read LEGEN-DEER.

'That's why I'd never heard of him. He doesn't exist.'

'Slow down a minute, Dad. How do you—'

'What do you think I've been doing in here? I've been trying to build a weapon, an antidote to the poison in the game.'

Phoenix couldn't believe what Dad was saying. Perhaps the last time in the labyrinth had unhinged him.

'John,' said Mum. 'What are you talking about?'

'Well, the joke's on me,' Dad went on, ignoring her question. 'I'm working for a phantom. As for the game—'

'Yes?' Phoenix asked. 'What about the game?'

'Forget it,' said Dad. 'Look you two, I know this is strange, but I can handle it. I've got to get on with my work.'

'But what work?' Mum demanded. 'If there is no Magna-com, then who are you working for?'

Dad pinched the bridge of his nose. He looked tired.

'I only wish I knew. But there is a way to beat the game. I'll find it, you see if I don't. I'm not working for Glen Reede and Magna-com any more. I'm working *against* them.'

'And you can work against them tomorrow,' Mum interrupted. 'John, this is scary. You've got me worried – both of you. I don't understand this game, and I don't want to, but you can't work night and day on it. Just take a little time to think about it.'

Dad stared at her. He was wavering.

'Please. For me and Phoenix. You've got to break off. Just for one night.'

Dad was a few moments coming to a decision, but eventually he nodded. For the first time in months the three of them felt like a family.

He was in the labyrinth again. He was running this time, sprinting through the tunnels slapping his hands on the walls.

They must be here. They've got to be.

The cheats – they were the only means of escape.

But the beast was in there too, and it was close behind. Phoenix could hear it shifting through the darkness, stalking him.

'This way,' cried a voice, a muffled male voice. 'Make your way towards me.'

A helping hand, thought Phoenix. But where? He eventually tracked the voice to a grating in the ceiling.

'Dad?'

But it wasn't him. It was a boy's voice.

'Surprise, surprise!'

'Adams! What are you doing here?'

'Don't you remember, Free Knickers? You invited me in.'

Then somebody else was speaking. The voice this time was female. Laura? Ariadne? It belonged to a woman all right, but there was no warmth in it. It crackled with hostility.

'Here comes the beast, boy. Say your prayers, because it's just round the corner.'

Phoenix stood beneath the grating, panting with fright. Where was it? Go forward or go back?

What do I do?

Then the question was answered. It was there in the gloom, the huge heavy head visible first of all, then its shoulders, then the powerful arms and the enormous club.

'Don't leave me here!'

76

He turned and ran.

'Dad, Laura, anybody. Help me!'

Then he saw Dad. He was on the other side of one of those gratings. Somehow, he'd wrenched off the metal grille and was reaching down towards Phoenix.

'Get me out of here!'

'Take my hands,' said Dad.

'Don't let me go,' begged Phoenix as the beast closed. 'Please don't let go.'

Dad was hauling him up through the hole in the ceiling. His legs were dangling, dangerously close to the beast. He could feel his breath, the spray of its saliva.

Hold on to me, for pity's sake hold on!

But suddenly Phoenix was falling, crashing to the stone floor in front of the beast, his breath dashed out of his lungs.

Dad! You let me go!

Phoenix was detonated from his dream.

'A nightmare,' he breathed, relief overwhelming him. 'Another nightmare.'

He looked around the room, half-expecting the beast to attack again, a dream within a dream. But it was over. He was safe.

For now.

He swung his legs over the side of the bed and sat there for a few moments, before checking on the time. It was half past two. On a whim, he walked to the top of the stairs. Was anybody still up? The light was on downstairs.

'Mum?'

He said it quietly, just in case she'd turned in.

'Mum?'

He walked downstairs and stopped outside the study. The ceiling light was off, but the computer screen was flashing. Had Dad left it on? Phoenix was about to return upstairs when Mum came out of the kitchen.

'Phoenix,' she said. 'What are you doing up?'

'I had a nightmare,' he told her.

She nodded.

'We've brought a nightmare into this house.'

Phoenix followed her into the kitchen. There was a fresh cup of coffee on the table, sitting next to the contents of an old box. There were a couple of notebooks, dog-eared and faded. A fan-shaped pile of curling black-and-white photographs looked intriguing, but he still wanted to know about Dad.

'Is he in bed?'

Mum gave a long sigh.

'He tossed and turned for a couple of hours, then he got up again.'

'You mean he's back in the study?'

Mum nodded.

'I did my best—'

She broke off, almost in tears.

'Don't cry, Mum. He'll be OK.'

Why did I say that? How do I know?

'It's not just John,' she said.

She held up a photograph, dated 1969. It showed a man in his garden. Obviously Greece. Phoenix noticed the family resemblance.

'Who's this? A relative?'

'Your Uncle Andreas. My father's brother.'

'Andreas? You kept him quiet.'

'They were twins. So close. They thought each other's thoughts, felt each other's feelings.'

'So where is he now, this Andreas?'

'He's dead.'

Mum fingered the notebooks.

'The family always thought he was mad. Now, I'm not sure.'

'But why did they think he was mad?'

'He saw things – apparitions, ghosts. He had always been bookish and painfully sensitive. He was also obsessed with ancient mythology. Then he started to believe those gods and demons were talking to him.'

Phoenix felt a shadow fall across his heart.

'It's all in his journal.' She looked into Phoenix's eyes.

'There is more . . . Something you should know. All his life Andreas suffered debilitating headaches—'

Phoenix started.

'Listen, Phoenix, I don't know if this has got anything to do with the game, but your grandfather gave me Andreas' journal when we moved from London. He didn't explain why. He just told me to keep it in a safe place, and read it *if anything happened*. I think I always had an idea what it was about. I've got a kind of instinct, a sixth sense.'

Phoenix smiled thinly.

'I tried to shut it out, deny the strange thoughts that came into my head. But when you started talking about Pan, I got the journal out and read it. It wasn't long before I understood the truth.

'Andreas wasn't mad. All I knew about him to begin with was that the family didn't like to talk about him. He was a kind of black sheep.'

She stroked the back of Phoenix's hand, as if to reassure him.

'There was only one exception, your grandfather. They were twins, remember. Even when Andreas started slipping away from the normal world, seeing those things, my father knew in his heart of hearts that he wasn't mad.'

'But what did Andreas see?'

Mum pushed the photograph across the table.

'Look closer. Dad pointed this out to me when he gave me the journal. It's quite a mystery.'

Phoenix frowned. 'I don't—'

'Look behind him, in the shadows of the wall.'

Phoenix's heart missed a beat. The image was hazy and ghost-like, almost lost in the shadows cast by an orange grove, but there was no mistaking those features. It was the guide to the game – Pan.

'It can't be.'

'The photograph has been in the family for years,' said Mum. 'I had shut Andreas out of my mind until you told me what was in the game.'

'But what happened to Andreas?'

'His obsession with his ghosts, his demons, got worse. In the end, the family placed him in . . . an institution.'

'A madhouse!'

'A hospital,' said Mum, correcting him. 'No, why should I cover up for what they did? That's exactly what those places were then. The family put him away. He saw things and they put him away in a madhouse. All the years he was there, he kept on telling anyone who would listen that there was a nightmare world, and its creatures visited him. Poor Andreas. He died in that awful place.'

Phoenix gasped. 'The demons got him.'

Mum smiled.

'No, there was a fire.'

'That's terrible. But why didn't you ever tell me about it?'

'Maybe it's because I was shutting it out. Nobody wants to believe in demons, do they?'

She paused.

'There is something else though.'

'Yes?'

'Don't you see? The legends, the headaches. I didn't want—'

'You didn't want me to go the same way?'

She paused before moving closer so that they were sitting side by side at the table.

'There is one last thing I have to show you.'

She picked up a photograph which had been lying face down in front of her and turned it over.

Phoenix felt his senses swim. It was a portrait of Andreas, aged fourteen. Phoenix didn't just look like him. They were identical.

It was like looking in a mirror.

13

'Like to tell me about it?'

At the sound of Laura's voice, Phoenix looked up. The 8.30 a.m. school run was an ordeal at the best of times. Adams made sure of that. This particular breezy morning it was about as much as Phoenix could bear. Dad still hadn't emerged from his study. The entire night had slipped away without him so much as putting in an appearance. Judging by the look on Mum's face and her edgy, brittle way of speaking, she was as unsettled by Dad's latest escapade as Phoenix was. He'd gone way beyond eccentricity this time.

'I don't think he's even had anything to eat,' she'd said at breakfast, returning from a fruitless attempt at getting him out. 'And he's locked himself in. I don't care how important his work is, he can't stay in there forever.' But even a second visit hadn't roused him. In the end, she'd had to go to work.

Phoenix stared at Laura. Her mouth was moving, but he hadn't heard a single word.

'What did you say?' he asked.

'I was wondering,' said Laura, sitting next to him, 'whether you wanted to talk. Something's obviously bothering you.'

'I'm worried about Dad,' he told her.

'How come? I thought everything was coming up roses. You know, with this wonder game and all.'

Phoenix frowned. 'It's the game that's the problem.'

Laura listened while he stumbled through a garbled explanation of the week's goings-on. But when she interrupted him for the third time to ask him whether he wasn't exaggerating just a little bit, he lost his temper.

'What is it with you, Laura? Don't you understand? Something really strange is happening here. Can't you even imagine anything out of the ordinary?'

'Don't have a go at me, Phoenix,' Laura retorted. 'None of this is my fault, you know.'

Their raised voices were a gift to Adams. He detached himself from his mates at the back of the bus and made his way up the aisle.

'What's this?' he asked. 'Trouble in paradise? Don't tell me you're falling out.'

'Clear off Adams,' warned Phoenix. 'This is none of your business.'

'My, aren't we touchy this morning,' sneered Adams.

Phoenix glared back at him. He reminded him of the ancient spirit that hounded a man to death and beyond, Nemesis. Adams was *his* Nemesis.

'Maybe you need another lesson, Free Knickers. You've forgotten how to talk to your betters.'

Phoenix lowered his eyes. He was still smarting from the humiliation of the fight.

'I don't want any trouble,' he murmured.

He'd got enough with the game.

'You should have thought about that before you started hanging round with Laura.'

'Oh, grow up Steve,' said Laura.

Adams chuckled and returned to his mates.

'Can't you ignore him?' asked Laura. 'Just say nothing.'

Phoenix nodded.

'Anyway, forget Adams. I want to hear the rest of your story.'

Phoenix turned his head and scowled in the direction of Adams.

'There isn't much more to tell. Only that Dad hasn't come out of the study for ages.'

'Are you sure? I mean, he has to eat, sleep, use the toilet.'

'You don't understand. He's obsessed.'

That's rich coming from me, thought Phoenix. Even now I would be tempted to play again.

'You know what you need,' said Laura.

'No, tell me.'

'You need a change of scenery. Get out of the house. Forget your problems for a while.'

'Yeah? So how do I do that?'

'You could come to my house for tea tonight. I told Mum and Dad I'd ask you, and they said it was OK.'

'I'll have to phone Mum,' said Phoenix.

'No problem,' said Laura. 'Just let me know later if it's all right.'

The bus was pulling up outside Brownleigh High. As he stood up, Phoenix felt Adams' elbow brush against him.

'Be seeing you, Free Knickers. Soon.'

Laura was right. He did need a change.

'That you, Laura?' shouted Mrs Osibona.

'Yes. Phoenix is with me.'

The Osibonas emerged from the kitchen wearing aprons. Phoenix smiled. Laura had told him about them, the way they did everything together. Like a pair of love birds, he thought.

'Glad you could come,' said Mr Osibona, wiping a hand on his apron and offering it to Phoenix.

'Thanks for inviting me,' he said as they shook hands.

'This came for you second post,' said Mrs Osibona.

Laura took the large bubble-pack envelope and turned it over. She examined the sticker on the back as her parents returned to the kitchen.

'If undelivered,' she read, 'return to Magna-com Products Limited, PO Box—'

'Magna-com!' exclaimed Phoenix. 'What are they doing writing to you?'

'Only one way to find out,' said Laura.

But as she started opening the envelope, Phoenix grabbed her arm.

'Laura, don't.'

'Don't tell me,' said Laura, 'you're expecting a monster to jump out at me.'

'Of course not,' Phoenix replied.

But she wasn't far off.

'Let's see what it is,' said Laura. 'I like presents.'

There were two items. She pulled out the small plastic case first.

'It's a CD.'

'Actually,' Phoenix told her, examining the black case, 'it's a computer game. *The* game.'

Laura pulled out a larger cellophane wrapper.

'It is the game,' murmured Phoenix, giving the Parallel Reality suit a wary look.

'So this is the famous game,' Laura exclaimed. 'At last.'

But before they could continue the discussion, her parents called them for tea.

'No no,' said Mr Osibona at the end of the meal. 'Don't get up. We'll do the washing up.'

'When did you order this game anyway?' asked Mrs Osibona. 'I didn't even know you were that interested in them, Laura.'

Laura gave Phoenix a sideways glance.

'I'm interested in this one,' she said, making her way to the family's PC.

'I don't think this is very wise,' Phoenix ventured, following her on unsteady legs.

'Why?' asked Laura. 'What can go wrong?'

Phoenix inspected the inoffensive looking disc and the rather more threatening Parallel Reality suit. Even now there was a little voice inside encouraging him to play.

'You'd be surprised,' he told her, resisting the temptation.

Laura was holding the disc thoughtfully between her fingers. After a few moments she put it down on the computer table and started to rip open the wrapper that contained the suit.

'I'm going to have a go,' she said excitedly.

Phoenix felt his throat tighten. His mind was suddenly loaded with rushing images from his last expedition into the game. It was alive all right, and it was expanding its territory.

He was beside himself. Seeing the plug he reached down and yanked it from the socket.

'Phoenix,' gasped Laura, 'What did you do that for? Imagine if my parents had seen you.'

'Sorry,' he answered, knowing his reply was bound to sound completely over the top. 'But I had to. It was a matter of life and death.'

'Oh, p-lease,' scoffed Laura. 'Don't be so melodramatic. You just don't want me to play your precious game.'

Before their disagreement could escalate, there was a knock at the door and Mr Osibona popped his head in.

'Phoenix,' he said, 'your mum is on the phone.'

In a day of uneasy moments, this was the most disturbing. Even before Phoenix picked up the phone, he knew something was wrong. Instinct.

'Mum, what does she want?'

The voice on the phone was breaking.

'Phoenix, can you come home? I'm worried.'

'Why, what's happened?'

'It's your dad. He's vanished.'

'He must have left a note.'

'I'm telling you, the study's empty and he's gone without saying so much as a word.'

Phoenix remembered the game and Dad searching feverishly for an antidote to its poison.

Retaliation? It couldn't be. It just couldn't.

'I'm coming home right now,' he said. 'Oh, and Mum—'

'Yes?'

'Stay out of the study.'

14

Fifteen minutes later Phoenix was standing outside the study.

'I'm going inside.'

Mum looked at him doubtfully.

'It isn't long since you were telling *me* to stay out.'

'We've got to do something.'

Mum sighed.

'But I told you. He wasn't in here.'

'No, I mean before he . . .' His voice trailed off. There was no point reminding her about the *bomb* Dad had been preparing for Glen Reede. She was worried enough as it was. 'Before he left.'

Mum fixed him with the same cautious look.

'What if . . . ?'

Phoenix nodded. They were both harbouring the same crazy suspicion. Phoenix wasn't sure what to expect, but in the event the room was a disappointment. Everything looked just as it had several days earlier. There were a few scribbled notes in his pad, but they were completely undecipherable. With the exception of the coffee cup with its dark brown dregs, it would have been hard to notice any differences at all. The computer was on, but there was nothing to see, just the screen-save program flickering away with its now familiar lines of numbers.

'We should have smashed down the door,' she said. 'Anything to get him out of here.'

'Don't blame yourself,' said Phoenix. 'It was his decision.'

Phoenix turned to go. That's when he noticed the box that contained the Parallel Reality suits.

'Hang on.'

'What is it?'

'I'm not sure yet. I've just got to check something out.'

He lifted a suit, then rummaged in the polystyrene packaging.

'What's wrong?' asked Mum. 'What are you doing?'

'That's funny,' said Phoenix.

It wasn't funny. It was unsettling. The way charged air before thunder is unsettling.

'What is?'

'Well, there should be two suits in the box, and there's only one here. And one of the points bracelets is gone. You didn't move anything, did you?'

'No, nothing. It's all just as it was. Except—'

'Yes?'

Mum glanced at the computer.

'There was one thing I wondered about. That was on, just like it is now.'

'The computer?' Phoenix sat down on the swivel chair in front of the screen, unease turning to panic. 'You mean you didn't switch it on? It was still on from when Dad was using it?'

'I'm not sure—'

'Think Mum, this could be important.'

The crazy suspicion was haunting them both.

'You don't think . . . No, John wouldn't be so stupid.'

Phoenix held his hand up.

'Bear with me, OK? Now, cast your mind back. Was there anything on the screen when you came in?'

'Just give me a moment. Yes, got it!'

He already had an idea what she was going to say.

'It was the palace,' Mum began. 'A bull's head symbol on the walls. The palace of King Minos.'

Her eyes widened, as if her worst nightmare had been confirmed.

'I knew it,' murmured Phoenix.

The labyrinth. Where the Minotaur awaits, hideous, bloody, brooding.

'It can't be,' said Mum. 'No, it's impossible.'

Phoenix lowered his eyes.

'With the game, nothing's impossible.'

That's when the phone rang. Mum flew to answer it.

'Oh, it's you, Mrs Osibona. Laura? No, she's not here. Phoenix, do you know where Laura is?'

'No, I left her at the house.'

In his mind's eyes he could see her, standing by the PC, itching to play the game.

'Yes, that's very strange,' said Mum. 'But Phoenix tells me she was still at home when he left.'

Phoenix was about to volunteer more information when he heard Laura's voice.

So you are here. You followed me.

He went to the front door and opened it, but there was no sign of her. Phoenix frowned. He wasn't imagining it. He *had* heard her voice.

'So where—?'

That's when his heart kicked. He knew where her voice had come from. The study – from the computer's twin speakers. She was calling to him from *inside* the game.

Moments later he was sitting in front of the screen with the Parallel Reality suit spread out on his lap. He was staring in disbelief at the pictures on the screen. What he'd thought about Dad, it wasn't a wild theory at all. It was true. Chillingly true.

'Oh, Laura, didn't I tell you not to play the game?'

There on the screen, Laura was racing up and down a deserted beach, crying out at the top of her voice.

'Phoenix. Anybody. Can you hear me?'

He ran his fingers over the suit. It was a nightmare come true. The game was alive. It could reach out. But it didn't just reach into the fabric of time and place, *his* time, *his* place; it fed on them. It looked for its players, played its little game of cat and mouse, then devoured them.

'Phoenix. Someone. Help me. Help me!'

Laura's voice burst achingly from the speakers.

'Please.'

Phoenix knew what he had to do. His fingers shaking slightly, he snapped the suit open and stepped into it. All the time he was pulling it on, he stared straight ahead, dull-eyed. Like a sleepwalker.

'Phoenix!'

He sat in front of the screen and made a decision. The game had Dad and Laura. Now it wanted him too. But he wasn't going into it as a victim. Somehow, he knew he could conquer it. He was going in to fight. He looked at the figure of the teenage girl running in circles on an unknown beach and he made his grim promise.

'I'm coming, Laura.'

He drew the balaclava-style mask over his head and plugged the suit into the PC. Mum had just hung up on an anxious Mrs Osibona when she happened to see him through the open study door.

'Phoenix, no!'

But she was too late. A split second later the room was empty.

BOOK TWO

———

The Book of the Legendeer

THE LEVELS

Level Nine
The Gorgon's Stare

1

This time there was no choice. Before Phoenix, flashing against the azure sky, was a menu. Only one option was highlighted.

Level Nine: *The Gorgon's Stare*.

No sooner had he selected it than he was lying face down, clutching at damp, heavy ground.

I'm back. Back in the game.

He scrambled to his feet and took in his surroundings. He was standing on a beach with the sea wind booming in his ears. He started looking around for Laura. He didn't have to search for long.

'Oh, Phoenix!'

She took a few steps towards him then stopped abruptly.

'Tell me I'm not going mad. We *are* by the sea, aren't we?'

'That's right.'

'But how? I don't understand.'

'It's the game, Laura. It's all part of the game.'

Then he remembered his warning.

'I thought I told you not to play.'

She didn't reply. She was reaching down, plunging her hands into the waves of the incoming tide.

'But this is no game. It's real water, real sand.'

'Or parallel water, parallel sand.'

Laura fixed him with a withering glare.

'I don't know what you're talking about, Phoenix,' she said. 'All I know is that we're on a beach somewhere.'

And I know where, thought Phoenix.

'Phoenix,' said Laura. 'I'm scared. This isn't fun any more. Just get me home.'

'That's the whole point,' said Phoenix. 'I don't know how.'

'Can't you just press a button, or something?'

'I only wish I could.'

Laura was losing her temper.

'You got me into this, Phoenix. Now get me out.'

'Just calm down, Laura.'

'Calm down! I'm lost in some crazy computer game, and you tell me to calm down!

A trill on the seven-reed Arcadian pipes brought the argument to an end. Phoenix heard a familiar voice. It was the guide, Pan. He must have been watching them from his vantage point, perched on a rock overlooking the beach.

'You!'

'Now, is that any way to talk to your guide through this troubled land?'

Laura was staring at his cloven hooves and the wiry hair that covered his legs.

'What's the matter with you, girl?' he demanded. 'Never seen a satyr before?'

She shook her head slowly, her eyes widening.

'Are you for real?'

'Is anything, my dear? Is anything?'

Phoenix decided to try a more useful question.

'Is this Seriphos?'

'Of course it is. It is the destination you chose.'

Seriphos, home of Perseus.

'I see your faculties haven't deserted you entirely. What did you expect after all the times you fled from the Minotaur with your tail between your legs? You've been demoted.'

He inspected Phoenix.

'Oh, I do apologize. You don't have a tail, do you?'

'All right, all right,' Phoenix snapped. He was feeling sensitive about his failures in the labyrinth. 'Cut the jokes. So I'm playing the part of Perseus? That's lower than Theseus?'

Pan nodded casually.

'That's what demoted means.' From somewhere, he produced a pocket dictionary. 'Yes, demoted. Put down. Now just look at this. Put down also means killed. Quite apt, really.'

'So what happens now?'

'You fight your way back up. I'm afraid you scored less than impressively on level ten of *The Shadow of the Minotaur*. You had more than enough chances, but you barely tested the beast. It is the top level, of course, and you did keep coming back for more, but you failed so level nine it is.'

'What's level nine?' asked Laura.

Pan frisked gaily.

'Let me show you a trick. Go on, I'm dying to do it.'

Laura shook her head. 'No, I want to know what's in level nine.'

'That's just it,' said Pan. 'That's the trick.'

'Oh, let him do the stupid trick,' said Phoenix.

'Thank you,' chuckled Pan. 'I know you won't be disappointed.'

With that, he began to sniff and snort.

'What's he doing?' asked Laura.

She got her answer instantly, and in the most dramatic fashion, as Pan drew a twisting serpent from each nostril.

'Oh, that's disgusting!'

Pan clapped his hands at Laura's expression of disgust. 'But the best is yet to come,' he announced.

Immediately his hair started sprouting dozens of snakes.

'Going to tell her, Legendeer?'

Phoenix nodded grimly.

'Not got it yet, Laura? It's Medusa.'

The serpents retreated into Pan's scalp as quickly as they'd appeared.

'Exactly, *The Gorgon's Stare*. If you want to try your hand once more in the lair of the beast, you must first conquer the Gorgon, Medusa.'

'So, to get back to the palace of King Minos, I have to complete this level?'

'That's about the size of it.'

'What about Dad?' Phoenix demanded. 'You mentioned my dad.'

'Reach the heart of the labyrinth and your questions will be answered.'

'So he is in here?'

'Complete the game, Phoenix Graves. There is no other way forward.'

Laura turned to Phoenix.

'Is he trying to tell us we can't stop it?'

Phoenix gave her a sad smile before turning to Pan.

'Let's get this straight,' said Phoenix. 'I'm here because I failed as Theseus?'

'Oh yes, you got that right,' chuckled Pan. 'The labyrinth's far too hard for a beginner. Whoever let you try was either wicked or stupid.'

The thought flashed through Phoenix's mind. Glen Reede or Dad. But whatever he thought of Reede, it wasn't fair on Dad. He wasn't stupid. It's simply that he was out of his depth, like any normal person would be.

'No,' Pan continued. 'It's the Gorgon's head for you, my lad, and even that's a tall order. You need a bit of practice before you're ready to slay demons.'

As Pan pumped invisible iron, Phoenix remembered his miserable defeat at the hands of Adams.

'Call it a workout,' said Pan, completing his exaggerated bicep curls. 'Sure you're up to it?'

'I'm not sure of anything.'

Pan threw back his shaggy head and roared with laughter.

'And you're the hero? Can so much really be resting on such frail shoulders?'

Phoenix frowned. 'Look,' he said, setting his curiosity aside.

96

'You may be a god, but there's no need to rub my face in it. Just give me a clue. Where do we start?'

'First,' said Pan, 'those clothes. So other-world, so Earthly.'

With a snap of his fingers Phoenix and Laura's jeans and tops were replaced by white tunics.

'Togas?' asked Laura.

'That's Roman,' Phoenix told her. 'Chitons.'

'You should fit in better now,' said Pan, inspecting his handiwork.

'I doubt it,' Phoenix replied.

'Meaning?'

'You may not have noticed, but there's the little matter of Laura being black. Won't she stand out a bit in Ancient Greece?'

'She could be Persian,' said Pan offhandedly. 'The Hellenes don't care about skin colour.'

'She still won't pass for Persian,' Phoenix countered.

'It's a vast empire,' said Pan. 'Say she's from foreign parts. That usually works.' He turned it over in his mind. 'Yes, it ought to get you by.'

'Get us by!' cried Laura. 'I don't want to get by. I don't even want to be here. I want to go home.'

'Home!' said Pan from his perch. 'That could be difficult. It may take some time.' He picked himself up and turned to go.

'What do you think you're doing?' Laura demanded, beside herself. 'You can't just clear off.'

Pan winked.

'Oh, can't I?'

Then he was gone.

'What are we supposed to make of all that?' asked Laura. 'I mean, is he real?'

'Beats me.'

'Just a minute,' said Laura. 'Somebody's coming.'

Phoenix squinted against the strong sunlight.

'There are two of them,' he said.

'How will we explain who we are?' she asked.

Phoenix wanted to say he was the hero, but he wasn't sure whether he believed it himself.

Phoenix shielded his eyes against the strong sunlight and watched the approach of the two men through the heat haze. Two spearpoints, two sword blades. At the sight of their weapons and the face-pieces that gave an inhuman look to their helmeted heads, he felt his insides begin to dissolve.

'We'd better hide,' he said. Then from somewhere he found the courage to stand his ground.

'No, maybe not.'

*That's right. I don't need to come up with a story. I'm Perseus. I **am** the story.*

'Perseus,' they shouted. 'You're wanted at court.'

'Court?' whispered Laura.

'This island of Seriphos is an unhappy land,' Phoenix explained. 'It is ruled with great cruelty by a tyrant king. His name is Polydectes.'

'Tyrant,' Laura repeated, raising her eyes skyward. 'I might have guessed.'

'Just try to keep mum,' he advised as the heavily armed men approached. 'Let me do the talking.'

The game was there to be won, but they couldn't afford any mistakes.

'Oh, don't worry,' said Laura, 'I don't want anything to do with this madness. It's all yours, thank you very much.'

The soldiers arrived, sweating under their armour and helmets.

I have to find the words.

'King Polydectes isn't happy about you disappearing like this. He demands your presence – now.'

Laura gave Phoenix a sideways glance. She was obviously impressed that he'd got the king's name right. He was tempted to tell her that he knew the story into which they had been plunged, but precious little else. Somehow he didn't have the heart.

'Who's this?' asked one of the spearmen.

'She's—' Phoenix remembered Pan's advice. 'A servant,' he explained, struggling to overcome the shake in his voice. 'Brought from foreign parts.'

He quite enjoyed the look of suppressed fury on Laura's face as he delivered the line. Servant! The main thing was, it satisfied the two soldiers.

'Well, let's be having you, young Perseus.'

They fell in line behind the two soldiers. Phoenix was wondering about a strange tattoo on both men's necks, when one asked him a question.

'Been up to any mischief today?' he asked.

There are questions which disarm you, and neither Phoenix's books nor his newly found intuition gave him a defence against this one.

'Mischief? What sort of mischief?'

The second soldier laughed out loud. His helmet tilted back, revealing the tattoo. An owl.

'What sort of mischief, he says! Drinking, brawling, carousing, your usual style, my laddo. What sort of mischief indeed! The sort that could see you locked up in the palace cells for ever and a day. I tell you, you've done it this time, you young scamp.'

Laura gave Phoenix an enquiring look, but he was stumped. He dug deep to discover what he was supposed to have done – what Perseus had done – but he came up empty-handed.

It was the first soldier's turn to make conversation. 'I don't think that mother of yours is doing herself any favours, either. I can't think of another woman on this island who would turn down King Polydectes' hand in marriage. She's brave—'

'Or very foolish,' his companion interrupted.

'Your mother,' Laura hissed. 'What are they talking about?'

'Not *my* mother,' Phoenix whispered back. 'The mother in the game – Perseus' mother. I'm just playing a part, remember. Never lose sight of one fact – this is all part of the game.'

Laura frowned. Phoenix squeezed her upper arm in a gesture of reassurance.

'Just trust me.'

The court of King Polydectes was less a palace than a fortress. Its forbidding battlements were guarded by sentinels carrying tall spears and massive, elaborately wrought shields. Scarlet banners fluttered from the ramparts. Ominously, black standards flew alongside them. The mark of death and mourning. As he followed in the footsteps of the soldiers, Phoenix could feel his legs turning to mush. It was one thing finding the words, one thing *playing* the hero, but heroes have to fight. The horse hair crests that nodded on the shining helmets of the soldiers only added to the air of menace. Phoenix took in the scene and remembered Perseus' mission.

How can I deliver the head of the Medusa? I'm just a kid.

The first guard broke in on his thoughts. 'There you go boy, take yourself inside. I wouldn't like to be in your shoes.'

That makes two of us, thought Phoenix as the guards brought them to the entrance of the palace.

'What are you waiting for Perseus? You know your way from here.'

Phoenix stared. I do? He took in the massive, hostile fortress. The monstrous battlements swam before his eyes. But it wouldn't have been wise to voice his doubts.

'Yes, I do.'

He led the way inside, out of the glare of the late afternoon sun. The gloom of the marbled interior rushed to embrace them.

'Now where?' asked Laura.

Phoenix looked around. There were corridors to left and right and a broader one still that led straight ahead. For all the dread that was mounting inside him, he had to sound in control. For Laura's sake.

'There.'

They were walking under an ornate archway. The crest at the centre caught his attention. The head of the Gorgon. He felt the reassuring chatter of the points bracelet as his score mounted.

'Yes, this is it.'

'But how do you know?'

He pointed up to the Gorgon's head, then to the huge doors.

'It's no broom cupboard, that's for certain.'

Laura smiled for the first time since they had entered the game.

'That guard,' she said, 'he said you'd done it this time. Done what?'

Phoenix shrugged.

'I just wish I knew myself.'

Time shuddered to a halt as they hesitated outside the doors.

'Phoenix?'

Her expectant look made him ache.

What if I let you down.

Then the inevitable guilt.

Like I did Dad.

He braced himself for his entrance and pushed. It was as if he had walked on a grave. The court of King Polydectes occupied a vast hall. Its dark, cavernous depths were lit by braziers that towered over the sentinels who were standing to attention around the walls. Carved reliefs displayed the three Gorgons, the sisters of evil who dwelt at the end of the world. The die was cast. Polydectes sat on a raised platform flanked by his bodyguards. He lounged on his throne, only his eyes shifting. He had a wolf's face, lean and clean-shaven, and it was no comfort that his black hair was greying slightly. Polydectes had the look of a ruthless hunter. Age only testified to experience, and cunning. But it wasn't the king who struck fear into Phoenix's heart. In the centre of the hall there was a long couch where a body lay, as if in state. It was the corpse of a youth his own age, anointed with oil, dressed and adorned with flowers, wreaths and bronze jewellery. The lifeless face, partly masked by its burial trappings, looked strangely familiar. For a moment Phoenix was convinced that he recognized its features. Then he dismissed the idea as quickly as it entered his head.

Don't tell me this is what Perseus has been up to?

A black shroud covered the corpse to the chest. Phoenix caught the eyes of Polydectes. The old wolf's gaze was flitting from the corpse to Phoenix and back again. The youth had died at the hands of Perseus all right. The game had already dealt him a losing hand.

I'm a—

'Murderer!' yelled an old man who had been standing by the body.

A woman, probably the boy's mother, rushed forward and raised her hand to strike Phoenix.

Only the intervention of a burly guard stopped the attack. Phoenix was aware of Laura watching him, but he stared straight ahead.

'Pray silence for the king!' bellowed a guard.

Phoenix watched anxiously as Polydectes rose from his throne.

'Well, young Perseus, serious charges have been laid against you.'

'Murderer!' the old man roared again. 'Lord Polydectes, I demand justice.'

The cry was taken up by every member of the dead boy's family. Phoenix shrank back, wanting to protest his innocence, but unable to utter a word.

'Justice! Justice!'

It was as if the whole thing was choreographed. Parts in a play, thought Phoenix, you're all playing parts.

Polydectes raised his hand.

'I weep for you and your loss.'

Weep, Polydectes? Since when did tyrants weep? Phoenix only knew about this king from the legends, but he already detested the wolf's face. And Polydectes had the false smile of a hypocrite and a cheat. Hatred flared in Phoenix's heart. For the first time, he felt ready to plead his case. Hatred was strength.

'There you have it, Perseus. Do you see the result of that temper of yours? What began as a tavern brawl has led to the death of a young man of good family. I have been patient with you for your poor mother's sake, but you must see that my hands are tied. A bereaved father craves justice.'

At last Phoenix found his voice.

Hatred is strength.

'Lord Polydectes,' he began haltingly, feeling his way. 'I am sorry for a family's loss, but I plead my innocence.'

'Innocence!' cried the dead boy's father. 'Half a dozen men saw you draw your sword. Half a dozen saw you strike and the point darken with blood. Assassin! Murderer!'

Clinging to what he remembered of the legend, Phoenix doggedly continued his defence.

'Let the son of Cronus, wide-browed Zeus decide my fate. I throw myself on the mercy of the gods. I call on the gods of high Olympus to weigh my life on their scales.'

Phoenix could scarcely believe his own words. It had taken a struggle to dredge them from the depths, but once found, they tripped easily from his tongue.

Polydectes joined the grieving family by the body. He snaked one arm round the shoulder of the sorrowing mother. It was a comforter's embrace, but the eyes of the tyrant showed through the flimsy pretence.

As if you care!

'There is only one penalty for murder in my kingdom—'

'Death! Death!' cried the mourners, right on cue.

'Aye,' said Polydectes. 'Death it is, but my verdict must wait. We are about to bury this victim. This is a solemn and a sacred act and I forbid any unseemly quarrelling during the rites. I will give judgement after the funeral.'

To the beat of a drum the funeral procession began to file out of the hall. Laura looked at Phoenix hesitantly. He simply held out his hand.

'What is all this?' she asked.

'The next episode in the game,' he told her. 'This whole level is devoted to Perseus. That's what Pan told us. The tyrant Polydectes wants to force the mother of Perseus into marriage. Only the hero stands in his way. Something tells me this is a put-up job. Polydectes is getting me out of his hair so he can go ahead with his wedding plans.'

'By sending you on an impossible mission?'

Phoenix nodded.

'Medusa.'

Laura shook her head. 'I keep pinching myself. I just need to wake up and I'll be home. Like Dorothy in *The Wizard of Oz*.'

'Forget it,' Phoenix told her. 'There's no Yellow Brick Road here. We're working in the dark, but this much I do know. Once the game has begun, we've got to play it to the finish.'

Laura stared at him.

'The game is insane, Phoenix. What can we do against all this?'

Something was stirring inside him. A strength and a knowledge given him by his love of the myths. But would it be enough?

'We think, that's what we do. No matter how terrifying it gets, it is still a game. There must be ways to build up our power. There will be cheats too. That's the point of the game. The player has to have a chance. What would be the point of playing otherwise?'

'Are you sure about this?'

No, not by a long shot, but he didn't tell Laura that. As the cortege made its way to the cliffs that overlooked the sea, the sun was beginning to set. Bats were flitting restlessly among the wind-twisted trees. Soon, they were proceeding by the light of blazing torches in the hands of the guards. Wispy showers of sparks were illuminating their way. Ahead of them, where the pall-bearers were climbing steadily to the highest point on the cliffs, an enormous pyre had been built. Phoenix couldn't help but marvel at the intensity of his sensations. A priest was leading the lamentations, addressing the crowd.

'Stand and mourn at the pyre of our poor, murdered son. With sacred honey, oil and wine I anoint him.'

He raised a knife above the shoulders of an ox standing tethered in front of him.

'With the blood of this animal I honour him.'

The knife fell. A few moments later the bloodstained hands of the priest were holding up the animal's heart. Phoenix smelt the woodsmoke and felt the breeze on his cheeks. The illusion of reality was stronger than ever. Terrifyingly strong. There was something else, too. The priest had the same owl tattoo on his neck as Polydectes' guards. Phoenix had spotted it when the old man raised the sacrifice above his head.

'High Olympus, accept our offering.'

Soon the pieces of meat were being roasted on the fire. The fat spat and hissed like a nest of vipers. Phoenix blinked as the flames caught and the acrid smoke began to sting his eyes. As the fire mounted higher and the sun sank in the sky, the funeral came to an end.

'What now?' asked Laura.

'I don't know.'

He had been too busy trying to solve a puzzle. What sort of cremation is it when they don't burn the body?

'Laura,' he asked, 'did you actually see what happened to the dead boy?'

She looked at him for a moment, then her eyes widened.

'You're right, they didn't put him on the funeral pyre. There's something very fishy about all this.'

'Yes, like a corpse who isn't dead, maybe.'

And an owl-tattoo that was being worn like the brand of a secret society. Some of the mourners also bore the mark. Before Phoenix could explore either mystery any further, a guard approached.

'Follow me, Perseus. King Polydectes wants to see you in his private apartments.'

They were following the guard when Laura tugged at his sleeve.

'Phoenix, look.'

The King's Chancellor was dropping handfuls of coins into the mourners' eager hands. The corpse – that partly disguised, but strangely familiar corpse – was the first to hold out his hand.

'He's paying them off,' Phoenix exclaimed. 'I knew it. The whole thing *was* a put-up job.'

'But how do we prove it?'

'Laura,' he said, 'this is the tyrant's court. He has absolute power. What he says, goes. We don't prove anything.'

The guard prodded them away with his spear. Minutes later they were being ushered into the king's presence.

'Who's this?' Polydectes demanded as Laura followed Phoenix inside.

'My . . . companion,' he stammered.

Laura managed a sarcastic comment. 'I'm a slave.'

The king looked unhappy about her interruption. The girl didn't know her place. No equal opportunities in this world!

'Mmm.'

Phoenix was the next to speak. 'You wanted to see me, Lord Polydectes.'

There was no shake in his voice this time. The fear was still there, but there was something else. Something that might prove even stronger. A sense of belonging.

That's it. I'm home!

'I like you Perseus,' he said, the oily delivery making a nonsense of his words. 'I would welcome you as a son. That is, of course, if your dear mother were to agree to my proposal of marriage.'

There was a noise to his left. From behind a heavy curtain a woman appeared. For a second Phoenix's heart skipped. Could it be? Had she read the note and followed him into the game? But it wasn't *his* mother.

Though she bore Mum a passing resemblance, this was Danaë, mother of Perseus. Phoenix remembered his own advice. Never lose sight of one fact – this is a game. He took the woman's hands and smiled. He felt he owed her something. Danaë looked back, drawn and unsmiling. Her pale eyes were troubled pools. Something passed between Phoenix and Danaë. He could feel her feelings. Fear of the tyrant. Horror at the thought of being his.

Polydectes cleared his throat and started to speak.

'The penalty for murder, as you know, is death. I am however moved by your plea for mercy. I also wish to spare your poor mother any anguish.'

Phoenix looked into Danaë's haunted eyes. He could feel her

disgust for the tyrant-king, her captivity. What he'd give to wipe the smile off the tyrant's face.

'You have thrown yourself on the mercy of the gods,' Polydectes continued. 'All that remains is to strike a bargain. Name the trial you will undergo to atone for your crime and I will accept your plea for mercy. And remember, only the greatest trial of courage can cleanse your sin.'

Phoenix didn't have to search his memory this time. Thanks to Pan, the legend was clear, and with it the next step in the game.

'At the end of the world,' Phoenix declared, 'there is a cave. In this cave dwell three monstrous sisters, the Gorgons.'

Danaë gasped. Her hands were gripping Phoenix's so tightly that the pressure was causing him discomfort.

'The Gorgons,' said Polydectes, licking his lips. 'You're aiming high, young Perseus.'

Phoenix saw the hunger in Polydectes' eyes. It filled him with terror, but there was something else. He was *alive*. Every inch of him blazed with life. I have to aim high, he thought. There is a game to be won.

'With serpents for hair,' he cried, his voice ringing boldly round the chamber of Polydectes.

'Teeth that can tear their prey in half and eyes so terrible that they can turn a man to stone, the Gorgons are a match for any hero. Do you agree, Lord Polydectes?'

The king's beady eyes were sparkling with delight. He could almost taste the boy's blood.

'Oh, I agree. I agree.'

Enjoy yourself now, Polydectes, thought Phoenix, casting a reassuring glance at Danaë. I won't forget this trumped-up charge, and that living corpse. You will live to regret your deception.

'Let's strike the bargain then,' he declared. 'Two of the evil sisters are immortal and can't be killed. I will bring you the head of the third, the horror-eyed Medusa.'

'Done!' roared Polydectes.

'On two conditions,' Phoenix said, interrupting.

Polydectes was almost beside himself. In one fell swoop he would have the hand of Danaë and be rid of Perseus.

'Name them.'

'There will be no marriage until I return.'

Phoenix read the tyrant's eyes. He knew the fate of all who had challenged the Gorgon. There would be no boy to return.

'Agreed. What is the second condition?'

'By delivering the head of the Medusa, I will have proved my innocence.'

Yes, and won through to the next level of the game.

'You strike a hard bargain,' said Polydectes. 'But I agree. Done! When does your mission begin?'

Phoenix broke away from Danaë and looked Laura straight in the eye.

'Immediately.'

'You depart this very night?'

'Tonight.'

2

On the other side of the monitor screen, there were tears in the eyes of Christina Graves. Her first thought was to destroy the computer, to smash it to pieces and end the nightmare. But she knew in the same split second that taking a hammer to it would solve nothing. The very idea of a game that swallowed its players alive was insane, but it had happened. Her son and husband were in there, lost among the mists of a bygone age. It was no accident either. She ran her fingers over the photographs and journals that told the story of Andreas' life. Destiny was at work here, and it was painting on a canvas much greater than her imagination.

What a performance! the numbers declared, unread and unheard, *Oh, you would have been so proud, my sorrowing Christina. That was your boy speaking. I actually felt like applauding. That's right. I wanted him to get the better of that old scoundrel Polydectes. It's been such a long time since I found a worthy opponent, and now it has come in the form of an unshaven boy! What were the chances? Do you know what I will do, Christina? I will let you see him. Now, weeping mother, look through the numbers and see your son.*

With that the screen cleared and there was a familiar figure on a desolate clifftop.

'Phoenix,' cried Mum, her face flooding with joy. 'My Phoenix!'

But Phoenix didn't hear. He had been sitting on the clifftop for an hour, maybe more, staring out to sea when Laura asked the obvious question.

'What now?'

The dark waves rolled in and Phoenix listened sadly to the boom of the wind and the crash of the tide. Salt mixed with woodsmoke and stung his eyes.

'Phoenix, what do we do?'

'I don't know.'

'You don't know!'

It had sounded good, all that stuff about returning with Medusa's head. In the king's apartment, carried away by events and swept along by his sense of destiny, Phoenix had actually believed it. The instinct had been strong in him. But here under a starry sky that sense of being home had drained away leaving only fear and uncertainty. He didn't feel one bit the hero. Sitting at a computer keyboard, he could be a giant. But this was different. He was a fourteen year old boy in a foreign land, maybe even a foreign world, no more than a speck of dust under those blue-black skies. What did he know about killing monsters? Demon slayer indeed.

'But you said—'

If there was one thing worse than Phoenix's realization of his own weakness, it was Laura's trust in him and the thought that he was failing her.

'I know what I said.'

He pulled at a loose thread in his tunic. It reminded him of a loose thread in another suit.

'I've always been the same. When I was little there was this ditch at the bottom of the garden. I knew I could jump it. I was special, you see. I've always had that feeling inside me. So I jumped. Guess what?'

Laura was way ahead of him.

'You fell in.'

'That's right, Laura. I fell in. That's me – head in the clouds, feet in the mud.'

'But you sounded so convincing in there,' Laura complained bitterly. 'We're supposed to go to the end of the world, aren't we?'

'Yes.'

'And?'

Phoenix stretched out both arms, as if displaying the vastness of the land and their own puny size. 'What do you see, Laura?'

'The sea.'

'And?'

'The sky, cliffs, a city. What are you getting at?'

He allowed his head to sag between his arms.

'Unless you're clairvoyant, or you've got an A-Z of ancient Greece handy, we've got a bit of a problem.'

'And that is?'

'The end of the world, I don't even know where it is.'

Phoenix had barely finished when the trill of seven-reed pipes and a loud cough behind him brought him to his feet. A familiar figure stumbled clumsily out of the velvet night.

'Pan, you scared me out of my wits.'

The usual mischievous grin, then a question.

'Am I to understand that you are lost?'

Laura took over.

'We certainly are.'

'Then look no further. I am here to serve you.'

Phoenix was ready to go along with the game, but Laura had other ideas.

'Serve?' she cried. 'And how exactly does that work? Let me get this straight. You're a god, right?'

Pan mulled this over.

'For the purposes of the game, yes.'

'And you made all this happen?'

'Now that,' said Pan, 'isn't strictly true. I am your guide. That is all.'

'All?' cried Laura. 'But you're a god. I thought you were superhuman.'

'Superhuman?' Pan chuckled. 'Now that's a thought.'

'What do you find so funny?' Laura demanded. 'We've been spirited away by this stupid game, and all you can do is laugh. Where are your powers? Can't you just magic us to the end of the world and get this over with?'

Pan scratched his scraggy beard.

'You must understand what you are dealing with. I have knowledge, some power too. But I am a very minor god. I am, like you, part of the game and subject to its rules. This is a world where gods exist, but it isn't *about* them. It is about the men and women who play the game and the ways in which they work out their destiny. I can't decide the outcome. Only you can do that.'

Laura stood up, waving her arms.

'But this is crazy! The game's about men and women, you say. We're kids. What are we supposed to do?'

Pan gave her a sideways glance.

'Simply this. You must play the game to its conclusion.'

'But can't you just call it off?' Laura asked. 'What if we say sorry?'

She shouted up to the sky.

'Can you hear me anyone? We didn't mean it. We just want to go home. This is all a mistake.'

Pan shook his head.

'It's no mistake. Phoenix is a player. He had his fair share of warnings on his little forays into the labyrinth, but he didn't take them. He was given every chance to walk away, but he couldn't leave it alone. He chose his path. This is his destiny.'

Phoenix listened. Pan was right. The die was cast.

'So what's the next move?' he asked.

Pan gave one of his unsettling smiles.

'Mine is the power of prophecy,' he said. 'I know your destiny within the rules of the game. You must slay the Gorgon, Medusa, and return with her head to the court of Polydectes. I can point the way. As for the rest, that is in your own hands. You must find the courage to make the kill.'

'But what's the point of all this?' cried Laura. 'Why can't we call it off? Why can't we just go home?'

Pan scowled.

'You forget, child. This is a *game*. Your minds must be as clear as a mountain stream. There have to be tactics, strategy, a gameplan. Most of all, there has to be thought. Though this

112

world may play the sweetest tune, you must never fall for its terrors or its delights, never confuse the game with reality.'

Phoenix had listened patiently until then. But that phrase, *never confuse the game with reality*, it wasn't right. He suddenly remembered the photograph of Uncle Andreas, and the strange figure in the background.

You, Pan. It was you.

'Use the myth as your pole star,' Pan ran on, unaware of the questions that were assailing Phoenix. 'It is an aid to navigate your way in treacherous waters. It is not, in and of itself, the whole truth.'

Phoenix was about to interrogate him about the ghostly apparition in a garden in Greece, when Pan cowered, as if spooked. He lowered his voice, eyes darting to left and right. There was a definite catch in his voice. Fear ruffled his hair like a spirit wind.

'My work is done for now. Prepare yourselves, the Olympian is coming.'

Phoenix looked out at the black sea breaking on the rocks below, the sea-spray mounting the cliffs, and shivered. He watched Pan scurrying away and turned his gaze out to sea.

I know who is coming.

'Laura, look.'

The clouds were parting and a startling figure was sweeping down from the sky. Though the form was human, its presence was immense. Its coming charged the air with a dark intensity. Laura must have felt it too because she shrank back.

Phoenix gave the presence a name. 'The goddess Athene.'

The goddess was armoured, her high-domed silver helmet reflecting the moon's glow. She was bearing a sword and spear. Hovering before them, she started speaking. 'You are Perseus?'

Phoenix remembered the way Pan had spoken. *For the purposes of the game, yes.*

He just said. 'Yes.'

'And you are pledged to bring back the head of the Gorgon, Medusa?'

113

'Yes.'

'Though it could threaten your very existence?'

A note of uncertainty crept into his voice.

'Ye-es.'

'The gods salute your courage, Perseus.'

My courage!

Phoenix remembered lying on his back, looking up into Adams' leering face. He remembered failing Dad.

What courage?

'If you are ready to accept your mission, I will furnish you with the tools.'

But for all the shaming images that haunted him, Phoenix knew that there was something else inside him. A steel, a conviction that he had a destiny.

'Then give them to me,' said Phoenix. 'I'll do my best to find the courage.'

As Athene led him to the mouth of a cave, Laura continued to hang back.

'There,' Athene announced, drawing back a cloth. 'Your weapons.'

She listed them. There was no need. Phoenix knew it the way a blind man knows his home. By a kind of second nature.

From Athene herself, a burnished shield in which to see a reflection of Medusa without having to look into her terrible eyes. Eyes that could turn a person to stone. From the Stygian nymphs, a pair of winged sandals, a helmet of invisibility and a magic wallet – a heavy leather bag – to carry the Gorgon's head. Finally, from Hermes, messenger to the gods, an adamantine sickle to kill Medusa.

As Phoenix ran his eyes over the weapons he heard the welcome chatter of the points bracelet. His score was climbing.

'There is no further help I can give you,' said Athene, turning to go. 'The winged sandals will take you to the town of Deicterion in Samos. There you will see representations of the Gorgons. Remember their images well, Perseus. Of the three foul sisters, only Medusa is mortal. Do not attempt to kill her sisters Stheno and Euryvale. Such a mistake would surely cost you your life.'

Phoenix nodded.

'From Samos you will journey to Mount Atlas. There you will find the Graeae, the sisters of the Gorgons. You will discover from them the whereabouts of Medusa.'

With that, the goddess was gone, returning to the storm clouds that were racing over the crashing sea. Phoenix was examining the weapons when he heard footsteps.

'You're armed,' said Pan. 'That's good. That's why you were chosen to play. The knowledge is strong in you. But by itself, even knowledge is not enough. It is courage above all that you must discover. When you fled the labyrinth, you exhausted almost every ounce of your life force doing it. If your courage fails again you lose. I hope you understand me well, I am talking about life and death. If you run this time you lose *all*.'

He closed his eyes and breathed the night air deeply, giving Phoenix time to take in this information. And time to prepare his question about Uncle Andreas.

'The only way to conclude the game,' Pan resumed, 'is to complete this level and return to Knossos to face the Minotaur. You have the time it takes for the moon to cross the sky thrice over. By then you must have Medusa's head or you may not proceed.'

Phoenix smiled.

'I understand.'

Pan turned to go.

'There is something.'

'Go on?'

'I would like to know how you came to be in a garden in my world fifty years ago.'

Pan stepped back as if suddenly unsteady on his cloven hooves. His eyes narrowed. It was some time before he managed a reply. 'It's a good question, but one I am sadly not at liberty to answer.'

'Not at liberty! What sort of answer is that?'

'It is the answer of a servant. Win the game, and you will have all the answers you want.'

'But—'

Before Phoenix could complete his sentence, Pan had vanished.

Laura followed him into the darkness, then asked, 'What was all that about?'

'All I know,' Phoenix replied, 'is that there's only one way out of here. We win the game, we find Dad and we go home.'

Laura pointed to the five things Athene had brought.

'How do you know they even work?'

'Pan seemed pretty impressed.'

'You're not telling me you trust that . . . that . . . that old goat?'

'I don't see we've got much choice.'

'But Phoenix, he got us into this. What if it's all his crazy idea? What if *he's* the enemy?'

Phoenix tried to explain. It was the way he'd felt ever since he first played the game.

I was made to play. I am the slayer of demons, the Legendeer.

He watched the expression on Laura's face. She still thought it was all an illusion.

Well Laura, you want proof? I'll give you proof.

'Phoenix, what are you doing?'

He started strapping the winged sandals to his feet.

'Oh no, you've got to be joking.'

'Stand back, Laura.'

He strode to the edge of the cliff.

There's only one way to make you believe me.

'Please Phoenix, don't do this.'

He stared down at the black, crashing waves and the jagged rocks. The boy that had been beaten by Adams wouldn't dare. The boy who had let go of Dad's hand would just sit on that lonely cliff forever. But he wasn't that boy. Not any more. He was becoming so much more. Laura was pleading with him.

'Please.'

I am better than that boy. I am reborn.

116

Stretching his arms up to the sky he threw himself over the edge of the cliff.

'Phoenix!'

He plunged into the darkness. The night wind was crashing against his face, stinging his eyes. The rocks were rushing up at him. So rapid was his fall, he could feel his flesh being tugged from his bones.

'Phoenix!'

Laura's voice was lost in the wind. It was almost over. He could feel the lash of the sea spray on his cheeks, the smack of salt on his lips. Then, as quickly as it had started, the downward plunge ended and he was sweeping upwards, light as a feather.

He was airborne!

'Can you see me, Laura, I'm flying!'

He swept high into the air, dizzy with the sensation of weightless flight.

'Didn't I tell you? I knew Pan could be trusted. I can fly.'

Then he was diving down, tracing circles round the astonished Laura.

'Still think Pan's a fraud? Well, do you?'

'I don't know,' said Laura doubtfully.

Phoenix dropped to the ground and walked forward. The score on his bracelet had rocketed to **550**.

'There's just one thing, Phoenix,' Laura said. 'What about me?'

'What about you?'

'You could call it a transport problem. We're short of one pair of magic sandals.'

Suddenly, Phoenix had the answer to everything.

'I conquered the night sky, didn't I? I defied gravity, didn't I? You simply take my hand and we'll cross the skies together. To the end of the world.'

Phoenix could see his destiny. It wasn't something beyond him, out of his reach, something decided by the game. It was his to grab hold of.

'I don't know, Phoenix. It looks dangerous.'

117

'Of course it's dangerous,' he cried. 'I've smelt the stench of death in the labyrinth. We have both heard the treachery in Polydectes' voice and seen the lengths he will go to to get what he wants. This whole world is dangerous.'

Laura was staring, wondering if Phoenix had gone completely mad. But he wasn't mad, he was reborn. Brownleigh, that stupid, boring little town, was dead and gone. That's right, thought Phoenix, this world of enchantment and monsters isn't the myth, *Brownleigh is*.

He raced across the wiry scrub grass to the cave where Athene had laid out her gifts. Bundling the helmet and sickle into the leather wallet and strapping the shield to his back, Phoenix strode towards Laura holding out his hand.

'Are you ready?' he asked. 'Ready for an adventure to the end of the world?'

3

The first thing Phoenix saw by the dawn light the following morning was the interior of the shepherd's hut where they had sheltered for the night. Laura was still asleep, her nose pressed deep into the yellowish-white fleece that she had wrapped tightly round herself. The second thing he saw made him jump for joy. Food. Fit for a king. Better, for a hero! Cheese, coarse brown bread, olives, grapes, oranges, even a jug of watered wine. Very watered. Their provider obviously didn't want them drunk! There was only the faintest scent of goatskin to give a clue to his identity.

'Laura. Hey, Laura. Breakfast is served. Courtesy of the very minor god, Pan.'

He watched Laura's eyes open at a squint. They were puffy with sleep, but opened wide the moment they registered the breakfast table.

'This is a dream. It has to be!'

'It's no dream—'

The moment the words were out of Phoenix's mouth, he realized something else.

No dream.

For the first time in days he had slept easy the night before, cradled by his new identity. The headaches had gone. The hero had woken refreshed. He sprang on to the table and started to dance around the platters.

Through a mouth stuffed with bread and cheese, Laura managed to speak. 'What's with you?'

Phoenix jumped off the table, grinning broadly.

119

'Those nightmares, Laura, about letting Dad down. I didn't have one last night.'

Laura was unimpressed. The next words she uttered were bristling with indignation. 'No wonder.' She pointed at the blazing light that was streaming through the open door. 'The nightmare is out there. Or have you forgotten where we are?' She swallowed the mouthful of food. 'And what we have to face?'

Phoenix poured two tumblers of wine, listening to the liquid cluck against the side of the earthenware cups. If what Laura saw through the open door was a nightmare, what he saw was a thrilling new world. *His* world.

He did his best to disguise his delight in his surroundings as he replied flatly, 'I forget nothing.'

Laura contradicted him. 'Oh, yes you do.'

'Like what?'

'Like what my parents are thinking. They'll be worried sick.'

Unsure how to reply, Phoenix made his way to the door with a bowl of bread, cheese and fruit.

'We should be in Deicterion by nightfall.'

'How do you know?'

He strapped on the winged sandals. Athene's gifts reminded him of his identity. He was the Legendeer now, in the form of Perseus.

'The moment I put these on I knew all sorts of things.'

'Such as?'

'Deicterion is a lawless town. A wild west frontier post, if you want. There will be bandits and cut-throats. Try not to look anyone in the eye. It wouldn't be a good idea.'

Laura shook her head.

'Can't I just wait here until you get back?'

'No. We have to stay together. You're here for a purpose just like me.'

'Oh, here we go again. What purpose?'

Phoenix mumbled his next few words like a guilty school-boy.

120

'You're here because of me. Remember the questionnaire I told you about?'

Laura gave a slow nod as if realizing what he was about to say.

'I named you as my heroine. You're not here by accident. It's fate. That's got to be it.'

Laura stood digesting the information for a few moments, then downed her wine without another word and walked to the spring to splash water on her face.

'I don't suppose Pan ran to a toothbrush?'

Phoenix laughed. The world of Brownleigh had been left behind, and with it the routines of school, home – and toothpaste.

'You'll have to scrub them with your finger.'

He gave her a few moments to finish, then reached out his hand.

'Are you ready to go?'

Laura gave his sandals an uncertain glance.

'Are you sure this is safe?'

'We flew together last night.'

It was as though he was born to fly. He skipped on wave tops and climbed halfway to the stars, taunting the wind and the wide-open sky. And all the while Laura was clinging to his hand with a vice-like grip.

'Yes, and my heart was in my mouth.'

Scared? Phoenix smiled to himself. You don't know scared, Laura. At the other end of the world three sisters are waiting. They know the hero is coming. They were born to await my coming. Their golden wings beat steadily in the putrid air. Their bronze hands stroke the petrified forms of adventurers who came before and were foolhardy enough to look into the Gorgons' eyes. The sisters wait and sniff the west wind like three hounds of hell. Their tongues hang out and loll against their leathery jaws. They know I am coming and they are ready, waiting. At the thought of the Gorgons, his nerves jangled. Terror and expectation were fighting inside him like wildcats in a sack. The old Phoenix told him to stay, to hide in a corner.

But I am better than that.

'Ah well,' he said at last, 'if you want to stay, then that's your choice.'

Laura's eyes sparkled.

'One thing though.'

'Ye-es.'

'You know the old saying?'

'No, but I'm sure you're going to tell me.'

Phoenix cleared his throat and glanced meaningfully at the flocks grazing on the hillside. 'Where there are sheep, there are Cyclops.'

'Do they really say that?'

He crossed his fingers behind his back.

'Absolutely.'

'And there are Cyclops round here?'

Time to lay it on thick.

'A single giant eye, two rows of bone-crunching teeth, a twenty foot tall frame of muscle and brawn. Yes, the brotherhood of the Cyclops roam these hills.'

Laura gave him a very long frown and took his hand.

'Let's go.'

It was the strangest thing. Phoenix didn't have to imagine Deicterion. He *remembered* it. The shadows of this new world must have been gathering around him ever since he was born. There was no rhyme or reason to it, but the hazy images were definitely memories. He was recalling things from beyond recorded time.

Deicterion was a walled town, its rough streets almost deserted as the braziers began to flare in the gathering dusk. An owl shrieked and swooped into a cypress grove, its hunter's song piercing the night. Phoenix thought of the strange tattoos.

'It looks quiet enough to me,' said Laura as they passed beneath its brooding battlements.

'Except for the owl.'

Don't let appearances deceive you, Laura. Remember Pan's

advice. It is a game, all a game. We won't leave this place without staring danger in the face. Perhaps even death.

'What was that?'

Laura was agitated, her head snapping round.

'We're being followed,' he told her, 'but you already knew that.'

Laura didn't want him to know that she was spooked by the quiet streets and the muffled footsteps behind them. She edged closer nonetheless. He liked the brush of her arm against his.

'I can't see anybody, Phoenix.'

He eased a rush light from its holder on a house wall. 'Take this,' he said quietly. 'When I tell you, throw it.'

He expected roughnecks spilling from taverns, brawling youths tussling in the streets, not this unsettling silence. The quiet gnawed at him.

'There!' said Laura. 'Something moved.'

Phoenix had seen it too. He slid the adamantine sickle from where it hung at his belt.

'It's a boy,' he whispered. 'Somebody our own age.'

Gravel scraped under the stranger's feet.

'Now!'

Laura tossed the rush light into the dark alcove. As it struck the ground, the glow revealed a familiar face.

'Adams!'

'What are you doing here?'

'You should know the answer to that. After all you invited me in.'

Phoenix stared. 'The questionnaire!'

Adams nodded. 'Clever boy.' A sly grin flitted across his lips. 'Not very alert though, are you? We've met before.'

Phoenix stared at him. Then the penny dropped. 'It *was* you. You were the walking corpse in Polydectes' palace.'

Adams crossed his arms over his chest and closed his eyes. 'It was a lovely service, if I say so myself. There's nothing like a good funeral, especially when it's your own.'

His eyes popped open and his expression changed. 'A

funeral, eh? Now isn't that a good idea. I let you off easily the last time we fought. Now it's for keeps.'

He drew a short, stabbing sword and struck out at Phoenix. 'Surprise surprise!'

Phoenix parried the blow with the sickle. Adams was taken aback by the speed of Phoenix's reflexes. Surprise yourself, thought Phoenix. We're not outside the school gates now. Adams lunged again, his blade once more clashing against the sickle. Phoenix saw the flash of dismay in his opponent's eyes and disarmed him with a slashing blow. Adams stared in disbelief as his sword clattered on the ground and shattered into fragments. It was a very different Phoenix he was fighting. Then with a guttural command, he scrambled away.

'Get them!'

With the start of the attack, Phoenix's senses had been sharpened. He was hearing intensely and feeling every twitch of his muscles. His brain filled with the sound of running feet. Armed men were spilling from the darkened doorways. Five, ten, fifteen. He'd got his roughnecks. In his lust for the kill, one man was outpacing the others. His unbuttoned jacket revealed a familiar blue mark on his throat, the owl tattoo. Phoenix's curiosity was aroused, but there was no time to worry about it. He had to bring the attacker down in the space of a single heartbeat. The adamantine sickle hissed as he wielded it, dealing the assailant a glancing blow. The youth crumpled to his knees with a groan, then fell at Phoenix's feet. He was elated by his success, especially when it added fifty points to his score.

'His sword, Laura, get his sword!'

'What am I supposed to do with it?'

There was no time for a martial arts lesson.

'Anything, just so long as it looks like you can do some damage.'

'But I don't—'

'Focus Laura. Remember, play it for what it is – it's a game.'

The next two assailants were upon them. Phoenix dropped the first with a swing of his glinting blade. The second hesitated and took the flat of Laura's sword in his face. The points bracelet was frenetically rattling up the score. Phoenix was starting to enjoy himself.

'Don't drop your guard,' he yelled. 'Just hit the target.'

In the melee, bodies were falling like cut flowers. The skirmish ended with raucous shouts and running feet.

'That was so easy!' Laura exclaimed. 'We're not fighting real people. We can't be. It's like cowboys and indians. Bang bang, you're dead, then everybody gets back up again.'

Phoenix wasn't so sure. He restricted himself to a neutral comment. 'We're clocking up points in the game. We can't just face Medusa cold. We have to build up our power.'

'But how do we know if it's enough?'

'Good question,' said Phoenix. 'I wish I had the answer.'

With that, he walked away.

'Where are you going?' Laura asked nervously.

'I have to take a look at something.'

He examined the first attacker. He wanted to see the tattoo. He turned the fallen youth's head to one side and inspected the mark. As he bent forward his victim groaned.

'He's coming to.'

The moment the youth regained consciousness, he gave a startled cry. Phoenix had the sickle at his throat.

'Tell me about this.'

The youth put his hands together, as if pleading for his life.

'This tattoo, what's it for? What does it mean?'

His captive began to stammer out a plea for mercy. 'Don't ask. Please don't. It will cost me my life.'

Phoenix dismissed the look of horror. He was play-acting, like the mourners at Polydectes' court.

'Don't be stupid,' said Phoenix. 'I just want to know about the tattoo. I've seen it before. What's it for?'

But before he could force a reply out of the youth, there was a loud thud from inside his throat. Hands reached for Phoenix and tore at his tunic.

'Please. Help me. I don't . . . want to . . . die.'

His eyes rolled back, showing the whites, and his head lolled.

The words gargled grotesquely in his throat. Just a game, Phoenix kept telling himself despite all the evidence of his eyes. It's just a game. But a hideous black bruise was spreading on the youth's neck and a trickle of blood was spilling from his mouth. This was all too real.

'I don't believe it,' said Phoenix, lowering the dead boy's head to the floor and drawing back. 'Something killed him.'

'What do you mean, killed him?' Laura demanded. 'It's cowboys and indians. Everybody gets back up.'

'Maybe that's what we thought,' said Phoenix. 'But this isn't faked.'

He stared at the body in horror.

'It's like a bullet went off *inside* him.'

Laura cut him short with a sharp cry. He felt her hands pulling at his tunic.

'Phoenix!'

Just as he was wondering what had got into her, an arrow head carved a path through the night air, smashing into a lintel and splintering the timber. Laura had reacted quickly, pulling him back with unexpected force.

The points bracelet clocked up an extra fifty points. His reward for cheating death.

'How many points would we have lost if the arrow had got you?' she asked.

'The lot,' Phoenix panted, a new understanding flooding through him. 'I'd be dead.'

All that time he thought he'd got the game sussed, he'd just been kidding himself. Forget cowboys and indians. His first feelings had been closer to the mark. It was real. The arrow head had been a lethal weapon. The game was for keeps.

'But—'

'Listen,' he interrupted. 'I don't get it either. OK, so a game's a game, but dead is dead.'

He tugged at the arrow's shaft.

'There's nothing virtual about this reality. Feel.'

While Laura examined the arrow, he pressed his back against the door.

126

'We're too exposed here,' he whispered urgently. 'Where's the door handle?'

Laura was the one who found it and they tumbled into the building. There was no time to take in their surroundings. The sound of running feet alerted them to another attack. Then a smirking face – Adams' face – appeared at a window.

'You did well,' he said. 'Better than I would have expected.'

Their fight was in both their minds.

'But it isn't over yet,' he chuckled.

Firebrands were being flung into the building, sizzling as they hit the floor.

'Surprise, surprise!'

By their flaring light, Phoenix and Laura began to make out the features of the room. Tall jars were stacked against the far wall. Phoenix plunged his hand into the nearest of them.

'A granary,' he told Laura. 'We're in a food store.'

'Phoenix, there. A back door. We can still escape.'

Too easy. Their besiegers would have had it guarded from the start of their attack.

'Listen Laura. They'll be expecting us to try the back way. When I give the signal, ease it open just the slightest amount then get right away from the door.'

'What are you going to do?'

He smiled. It was an unsteady smile. He was out of his depth but learning fast, drawing on the memory that couldn't be a memory, picturing sword-play in a quiet grove.

'I should have thought of this earlier.' He took the helmet of invisibility from the leather wallet and put it on, praying it would work. Hauling a grain jar over to the nearest window, he prepared himself for battle.

'Now!'

As fingers squeezed round the door Phoenix used the jar as a stepping stone up to the window sill and jumped down into the alleyway. The sickle did its work again, leaving the enemy, who hadn't even seen him, face down in the dust. The helmet worked.

'Phoenix!'

127

He reached the half-open door to see three men closing in on Laura. She was swinging the sword and backing off. They were enjoying the sport. Time to make an entrance.

'If it's me you're after,' he announced, 'then I'm here.'

The trio span round. Phoenix took pleasure in their confusion. They made for his voice but they were stabbing thin air. Under the cover of invisibility, he struck once, twice, three times with the sickle. With each cut of the ferocious blade, the points display registered another score.

'Let's go, Laura.'

They fled down the main thoroughfare of Deicterion, expecting more attacks at any moment. But none came. A hush descended.

'Why did they give up?' Laura asked. 'We didn't get them all.'

Phoenix was none the wiser. But give up they had. It's as if they had wanted to bring them to this place. Anxiety mounted inside him.

He slid off the helmet.

'I don't like this, Laura.'

She was just as jittery. Unable to believe the fight was over she made her way to a corner – and screamed.

Phoenix gazed upon the hideous faces looming towards them and breathed a sigh of relief.

'It's all right, Laura, they're not real. This is what we came for.'

In the stone walls of the town, three huge reliefs had been carved, matching the ones at Polydectes' court.

'The Gorgons.'

He had seen his share of illustrations of the legends, of course, and made his own sketches. But none were ever anything like this, not even those at Polydectes' palace. There was so much more detail. Each of the sisters had the body of a woman, but resting on a serpent's tail instead of legs. They were winged and their hands were armoured claws. Their hair was set in ringlets made of living, writhing snakes. But it was the face of the Gorgon that was the site of its terror. She had tusks like a wild boar and there was something that reminded him of the Minotaur. She also had the killing teeth of a big cat, a lion or tiger. A swollen rope-like tongue spilled from her mouth. But there was one detail that couldn't be shown in the giant carvings – her eyes. The sculptor hadn't even made an attempt to portray the eyes that could turn a man to stone. He had left his creatures eyeless.

Beneath each of the sisters, a name was carved. Stheno, Euryvale and Medusa.

4

Some hours into Christina Graves' lonely vigil at the computer she made a discovery. While watching Phoenix sitting on the clifftop, she happened to consult her watch. Seven-thirty. She observed the arrival of the goddess, the night spent in a shepherd's hut, the fight at Deicterion. Then she looked at her watch again. Still seven-thirty. She shivered right down to the marrow of her bones. It had to be a mistake. The watch had stopped. But she knew that was too simple an explanation. The clock on the wall registered exactly the same time.

'Stupid woman!' she declared after a few moments. 'Of course, it's seven-thirty in the morning. I've been up all night.'

But no sooner had the thought crossed her mind than she was forced to think again. Darkness hadn't fallen at all. She hadn't had to switch on the light.

'But this is—'

While one part of her was trying to come up with a rational explanation for the vice-like stillness around her, another – the deeper part – had raced ahead to a more incredible one. She walked around the house, trying to disprove her own suspicions. But her first intuition had been right. Not only had her watch stopped at seven-thirty. So had the hall and kitchen clocks, the bedside alarm and the digital displays on the micro-wave, oven and video. She even switched on the TV, only to see Homer Simpson, hands locked around Bart's throat forever.

'I'm going mad.'

She glanced out of the window. A scream froze in her throat. Everything was caught in a freeze-frame. Cars, people, clouds,

130

leaves, everything trembling on the cusp of suspended time. She tried the door. The handle and lock were jammed, sealed in that single, timeless moment.

Seven-thirty.

She had no choice but to return to the computer where the screen saver had clicked on, launching the endless rows of perplexing numbers across the screen.

Doing nothing to hold back her tears, she pressed her right hand against the monitor and sobbed out her pain. She was lost – just like John and Phoenix.

Maybe you are beginning to understand. There is only one time. The time of myth. It is your time, the time so carefully calculated down to a fraction of a second by sophisticated atomic devices, the time displayed on millions of clocks, that is imaginary now. The game is real, your world a dream. Time will move forward only when I will it.

It was noon next day before Laura and Phoenix reached the foothills of Mount Atlas. Another night had passed without dreams, without the labyrinth. Most of all, without fear. Curious, thought Phoenix, I've started to realize just how deadly the game is, and I'm not scared. I was born to complete this journey. The greater the fear, the greater the reward in facing it down. The same world that is making Laura so angry and afraid is allowing me to breathe again. For the first time since he had arrived at Brownleigh, furious at having to leave London, he felt truly alive.

'Looks like Pan got here before us,' he remarked, indicating the feast of meat and fruits laid out on a bronze table.

Laura was looking at the inviting fare, but she didn't rush forward like she had the first time.

'Something wrong?'

Laura ran a hand over her face.

'I need some answers,' she replied, unhappiness clouding her voice.

You and me both, thought Phoenix. I am the adventurer, the hero, the Legendeer, but I have entered a vast and very black cavern armed with the smallest of torches. For all my sense of belonging and excitement, I am part blindfolded. There is so much more darkness than light.

'What is all this, Phoenix? First it's a game, then it's real. The fight we were in, did we hurt those people? Was it cowboys and indians, or what?'

She waved her arms at the vastness of the sky. 'Somewhere out there my parents are worrying themselves sick about me. And I'm worried about them too.'

Phoenix lowered his eyes. His too.

'Sorry Laura, but I just don't have any answers.' He remembered the lifeless eyes of the youth he'd been interrogating, the gathering pool of blood pillowing his head. 'One thing we've both learned, you can't trust the game. This is a cruel world. Terrible things happen here.'

Laura sat heavily on a grassy knoll, resting her arms on her knees.

'Do you have to tell me something I already know? I just want to understand what's happening here. Did those people really die?'

What did Pan say? For the purposes of the game, yes.

'They died.'

Laura had been asking more in hope than belief.

'But it was too easy. Are you sure that sickle thing really works? I mean, back home they have war games. They use paint guns and stuff. Even grown men do it.'

Phoenix gave a scornful laugh.

'Paint guns, eh?'

He produced the sickle and brandished it to show the glint of its razor's edge.

'Set me a test.'

Laura looked round.

'That tree.'

One stroke of the blade and there was nothing but a stump where the sapling grew. Phoenix found himself laughing out loud.

'What tree?'

He walked over to the bronze table. Suddenly, there was a

storm inside him. Laura wasn't the only one who was worried. Phoenix wanted to smash things, tear them down.

'Want another demonstration?'

He brought the sickle down hard on the bronze table, making Laura jump. As it split, the plates of food slid to the centre.

'Satisfied?'

He glared at Laura, then seeing the look on her face, he immediately regretted his show of temper. He'd started acting like Adams.

'I'm sorry.'

She accepted the apology with a brief nod. Then there was another question.

'What about Steve Adams?' she asked. 'What's he up to? If all this is real, then he could have got us killed.'

'I do have an explanation,' Phoenix told her. 'Adams said it was the questionnaire that brought him here. He must have been sent a pack of software, just like you. Now the game is following my instructions to the letter. Me as the hero, you as my heroine, Adams as the villain. And Dad—' He felt a tug of regret. 'I put his name down too. He'll be here somewhere.'

'This is really hard for me, Phoenix. You fit in here. I don't.'

Fit in. Yes, he did. He *was* the Legendeer.

'You're doing just fine, Laura,' Phoenix told her. 'The way you handled that sword. The way you saved me from that arrow. The way you've kept your nerve all along.'

He didn't know how to tell her, but ever since they'd met their hearts had been beating to a single rhythm.

'I'd be lost without you.'

She smiled.

'Let's eat.'

A few moments later Phoenix was pointing out their next destination with a crust of bread. He pictured the inhabitants of the mist-shrouded slopes. The Graeae, sisters of the Gorgons, but bearing no resemblance to the snake-haired predators who lurked in poisonous mists in a cave at the end of the world.

Three Gorgons – powerful, savage, unconquered. Three Graeae – withered, ancient, wretched.

The Graeae were the wasted remnants of their former selves, little more than bags of bones. They lived their lives bickering constantly, forced to share one eye and one tooth. Maybe they dreamed of their sisters and envied them the terror they stirred in the hearts of men.

'But why do we need them?' Laura asked.

'Nobody has ever returned from the Gorgons' lair to tell of its whereabouts,' Phoenix explained. 'Only the Graeae can set us on our way.'

'But why would they betray their own sisters?'

'Because,' he answered, 'without the eye they are doomed to eternal darkness. Without the tooth they will hunger forever. We have to steal the only things that are precious to them.'

Laura gave him a nervous look.

'This is going to be grotesque, isn't it?'

'Very.'

He could almost hear the air shuddering in Laura's throat.

'Then we'd better get it over with.'

The image Phoenix had of the Gorgons blazed up again in his mind. He circled the summit of the mountain slowly, peering down through wispy clouds. There was a warning here. Laura clutched his hand even tighter. 'Something wrong?'

'I don't know. It's this picture I keep getting in my head. No . . . I've got it. Of course, they're onto our scent!'

The Gorgons were sniffing the wind, that's how they knew Laura and Phoenix were coming.

And the Graeae too, if he wasn't mistaken.

'We've got to land downwind of the creatures.'

Laura gave him a wary look. 'If you say so.'

They edged down the slope towards the three marble thrones of the Graeae.

'There!'

It was them, all right. Three bags of bones, husks of living things. Toothless, sightless, reduced to arguing over a single eye and a single tooth, they scrabbled and clawed at each other, demanding their turn to see or to eat. One of the twisted beings reared suddenly. 'Sisters, what was that?'

'Nothing. I know you, you crone. You didn't hear a thing. It was just a ruse to steal away the eye.'

'Calling me a liar, are you, you pathetic worm? It *is* my turn with the eye.'

Their fight resumed.

'Cheat!'

'Liar!'

But then their squabbling broke off again.

'No, there it is again. He's coming, sisters. The one who was prophesied – the boy of Seriphos.'

Phoenix glanced at the startled Laura and winked. He was so alive.

'Skirt round to their left,' he whispered. 'When I give the signal, I want you to create one almighty commotion.'

Laura bit her lip, as if he'd asked her to balance the whole world on her thumb, and crept away through the undergrowth. She'd had enough stomach for the street fight. This was a different matter.

Phoenix, on the other hand, was in his element. The part he was playing *was himself. I'm coming, ladies. It's I, the boy of Seriphos.*

The three of them were raised on their haunches, sniffing at the breeze. And all the time they were snatching the eye, taking turns at scanning the mountainside for any sign of Phoenix.

'You'll never find the cave of the Gorgons,' cackled one.

'No torture will break we three,' said another. 'There is a blood bond here.'

Laura had got behind them, averting her face. She couldn't bear to look at the malformed sisters. Phoenix drew the sickle and slipped the shield from his back, turning it upwards like a dish. Then he raised his arm and dropped it immediately. Laura started dancing, shouting, yelling for all she was worth.

The Graeae were falling over themselves to get a look at the strange girl.

'Who is it?'

'What's she doing?'

'Where's the eye? Let me see.'

The eye was being passed from hand to bony hand. Phoenix watched as one twisted claw reached out, then he leapt forward.

'Mine, I think.'

With a flick of the wrist, he used the sickle like a spatula, tossing the eye and the tooth into the air.

'Thank you kindly.'

He watched the eye roll round the shield and come to a rest in the middle. The tooth rattled beside it.

'Now ladies, time to bargain.'

The Graeae were thrown into a frenzy.

'Give them back!'

'You'll pay for this, boy.'

'Wait till my sisters get hold of you. They will rip you open like a fig.'

As Laura shrank back in disgust Phoenix waited for the sisters' anger to ride itself out.

'Now,' he said finally, when they had exhausted themselves with their raging and cursing. 'The location of the Gorgons' cave, if you please.'

'It'll do you no good.'

'I don't know why you're in such a hurry, boy.'

One rubbed her scrawny stomach.

'The sisters will give you a fine welcome.'

'Munch you.'

'Crunch you.'

'Gobble you up.'

Phoenix rolled the eye and the tooth round the shield.

'Hear that? I could deposit them half a world away. Mmm, I quite like the idea. You've got good hearing, haven't you? Imagine, you could listen to them as they fall into the sea. Plop! Such a lovely sound.'

Another frenzy, then the Graeae resigned themselves to defeat.

'Very well, we'll tell you boy, but little good will it do you.'

'Are you in such a hurry to die?'

He'd had enough of their abuse.

'The location, please. Now! Or you'll never see the eye or the tooth again.'

'I'll tell you,' said one. 'On one condition. I have the eye first.'

'No,' shrieked her sister. 'Me, Me!'

More squabbling, then bit by bit they spat out the directions to the Gorgons' lair in the Land of the Hyperboreans. Satisfied with his day's work Phoenix tossed them their prizes. 'Here.'

The last Laura and Phoenix saw of the Graeae was a tattered mass of rags, scrambling in the mud and the dust, and all for an eye and a tooth.

Night fell once more and Phoenix was at peace with himself. He wasn't afraid. His nightmares had gone. The headaches too. His lifelong torment was over. A meteor flashed over the mountain tops. There was a silence, completely unbroken by any sound except the scrape of the crickets. Until Pan put in one of his appearances, that is. Phoenix made himself a promise.

This time you don't get away without telling us the truth.

You're going to answer my questions.

'It's about time you turned up,' said Laura.

'A profitable day?' asked Pan.

'If you mean, have we found the cave, the answer's *yes*.'

'That's good,' said Pan. 'That's very good. It keeps the game going. Let's see your score.'

He examined the bracelet.

'Very impressive. Here, a present for you.'

He handed something to Laura.

'A flare? In ancient Greece?'

'You forget,' said Pan. 'This isn't Greece. At least, it is one possible Greece. This is the world of the game. And, as Phoenix

137

has already discovered, you're allowed the odd cheat. That's what makes it all so entertaining. It's the wobbles that make the high-wire artist interesting.'

Pan sidled up to Laura and laid his head against her shoulder.

'Do you like adventure, my pretty?'

Laura flinched at his touch. He grinned and sprang back, producing a knife and holding it to his own throat.

'Back off,' he barked in a Chicago-gangster voice, 'or the goat gets it.'

Phoenix stared. What is this? Maybe Laura's right. He isn't what he seems. Laura simply shook her head at Pan's antics. Then the pair of them gasped. The blade that Pan had pressed against his own throat had produced blood, a single scarlet trickle stringing into the briar-work of hair on his chest.

'Stop it,' said Laura. 'You're making me sick.'

'Just high spirits,' said Pan, staggering.

'You're drunk!' exclaimed Laura.

'A little tipsy,' said Pan, 'but that's my nature. We can't escape our nature, can we Phoenix?'

Phoenix could only stare, wondering what he meant.

Remembering the flare, Laura gave it the once-over and shook her head. 'But what am I supposed to do with it?'

'I'm sure you'll find a use for it. I hear it will illuminate the blackest night.'

Phoenix let him prattle on for a while then launched himself into his questions.

'What does the owl mean?'

Pan blinked, clearly taken by surprise.

'You're an intelligent boy,' he said, recovering himself. 'The owl is the symbol of Athene.'

'I know that,' Phoenix retorted. 'I mean here, in the game.'

'Now what do you think it is?'

'Oh no,' Phoenix warned him. 'You're not fobbing me off. You owe us an explanation. What's going on?'

Pan inspected his filthy, jagged fingernails casually.

'The world is turning. Stars flash and mortals wonder.'

138

'Cut it out,' snapped Phoenix. He drew the symbol in the dust, the perched owl. 'I saw it on some soldiers.'

'And that priest,' Laura added.

'And the boy fighter in Deicterion.'

Pan was acting stubborn. 'Then ask him.'

'I can't. He's dead.'

Pan yawned. 'Very well. It can't do any harm. The owl belongs to the game, and if you bear the mark of the owl then you too belong to the game. Surely you've worked it out by now. There is a world here which dances to one man's tune. There is but one Gamesmaster. His pawns do as they are told. By terror or by bribery, they do the bidding of their master.'

'And if they refuse?'

'Then they must wear the mark of the owl. If they dare defy the Gamesmaster's will again—'

'They die.'

Pan nodded. 'It is the way of all flesh.'

Pan made as if to go.

'One more thing,' said Phoenix. 'Tell me, Pan. Tell me about Uncle Andreas.'

'Andreas,' said Pan thoughtfully. 'Now I haven't heard that name in such a long time.'

'You visited him,' said Phoenix, pressing him. 'I want to know why.'

Pan's dark eyes blazed, stabbing deep into Phoenix's soul, branding it with the stamp of fear. 'If you know Andreas,' he spat, 'then you will find the answer inside yourself. You only have to look.'

With that, Pan stole into the night.

5

Next day, Phoenix and Laura rose at dawn and set off to complete their journey, heading westwards into the Land of the Hyperboreans.

Phoenix could feel Laura's eyes on him. 'Nervous?'

He nodded. It was an unnecessary admission. There was no disguising hands that were moist with perspiration. *Somewhere among the dismal mists of these endless grey hills the sisters are scanning the sky and sniffing the air. They are making themselves ready, waiting for me.*

As he descended with Laura through dense, reeking clouds he felt something, a tick-tick-ticking against his wrist.

Laura sensed his concern.

'What's wrong?'

Phoenix was staring in horror at his points bracelet. 'This is impossible!'

The display was chattering away as their score went into freefall.

'We're losing our power. Our points total is being wiped out.'

'But why? I don't understand.'

Phoenix found himself looking around, as if expecting somebody to pop up and give him an explanation. It didn't make any sense. They weren't under attack. Neither of them had been hurt. So how could they be losing points? Eventually the fall in the points score slowed, then stopped tumbling altogether.

'What have we got left?' Laura asked.

'It's bad news,' Phoenix told her. 'We're down to a few hundred.'

'So we're—'

'In the red zone. Mortal danger.'

But why? He shivered, as if aware that something terrible had happened.

'Are you all right, Phoenix? You look awful.'

'I feel awful. I mean, to have lost a score as big as that. From hero to zero. And without any sort of fight. It took the whole skirmish at Deicterion to build it up. What's done it? I mean, what can be worth the lives of a dozen street fighters?'

What indeed? Phoenix imagined the street fighters thrown into the pan of a giant scales. But what could be balanced against them?

'Oh no, it can't be.'

'What?'

'Dad,' said Phoenix. 'Reede's killed him.'

'Reede?'

'Glen Reede, I told you. It's him, or whoever's in control of this crazy game. It has to be. He's killed Dad for working against it. For preparing his bomb.'

'Phoenix,' said Laura. 'Calm down. Number one, you don't *know* he's dead, and number two . . .' Her voice trailed off.

'Go on,' said Phoenix. 'What's number two?'

'Let's face it,' Laura told him. 'We're not even sure any of this is real. What if—?'

'What?' Phoenix demanded. 'It's all a dream.'

He knew better. He could still feel the clash of steel in the fight at Deicterion. The legend was real. In fact, it was the only thing that was real any more. They were living in a world of legend.

'Think you're going to wake up like Dorothy in *The Wizard of Oz*? Think you're going to click your ruby slippers and fly away home? Grow up Laura, you saw that fighter in Deicterion. That wasn't cowboys and indians. He was dead Laura, and he was going to stay dead. We're playing for keeps.'

141

Then the world that had once been everything, was nothing. A dead ball of clay. Pointless.

'Dad,' he groaned. 'This is all my fault. I gave him the idea for the game. And I let him go.'

Laura shook her head and walked to the edge of a crag. She made a brave attempt at changing the subject.

'Do you think it will affect the mission, losing all those points?'

'It must do. All the points we'd built up, they were bound to help us. They were a cushion against disasters. With that score under our belt, I was on fire. I really was the Legendeer. Now—' He passed his hand over his face. 'I just don't know.'

'So do we go on?'

Phoenix deposited the shield and leather wallet on the ground.

'Looks like there's no choice. We have to fulfill our mission. Dad's life depends on it. If—'

If he's still alive.

'Ours too, I expect. Maybe a lot of others besides.' Then everything was coming together. His sense of destiny, his growing power, his rage to fight back. 'So let's prepare ourselves for battle.'

But when Phoenix loosened the drawstring on the wallet, he cried out.

'What now?' murmured Laura.

'The helmet of invisibility, it's gone.'

'It can't have.'

He passed her the wallet.

'See for yourself if you don't believe me.'

Phoenix closed his eyes and saw his destiny. Somewhere close by the sisters were waiting, licking their lips and sensing the hero's setback. Their golden wings glowed with satisfaction. It would soon be over.

We're waiting, boy. Come and do your worst.

It was Laura's turn to despair.

'But it doesn't make sense. You slept with it under your head like a pillow. Nobody could have taken it.'

142

Phoenix turned his face towards her.

'The game took it.'

'What, you mean Pan? I never trusted him.'

'No, not Pan. The game was always much more than any one player. It's playing with us. I don't understand it yet, but I know that the points don't lie. We've suffered a defeat. The helmet is the price we have to pay. It's too much, Laura. It's all too much.'

Laura gave the wallet one last inspection.

'What's this? Oh, I might have guessed!'

'What is it?'

She handed Phoenix a note. *Surprise surprise*.

'It wasn't the game, at all,' she cried, seizing on the scrap of paper. 'Don't give up, Phoenix. Don't you dare give up. It wasn't destiny. It was Adams. He did this.'

Phoenix watched Laura. She was trembling with anger.

'Maybe I don't know much about fighting monsters,' she said. 'And I don't know what makes this stupid world tick. But I do know this. Adams is human, and we can fight him.'

'I don't think there's any choice about the matter,' said Phoenix, subdued.

He felt another click on the bracelet. Five more points gone.

'This is worse than I thought,' he murmured.

Laura didn't speak. Instead, she waited for him to explain. For all her stubborn rage, the avalanche of setbacks was getting to her.

'It's something Pan said,' Phoenix told her. 'We don't have forever to get the head of Medusa.'

'So how long *have* we got?'

Phoenix repeated Pan's words. 'By the time the moon has crossed the sky thrice over. That's tonight.'

Five more points clicked away.

'Do me a favour,' he said. 'Count to ten.'

Laura had just reached ten when the score fell another five points.

'I was right, the game's being timed.'

143

Dazed by the turn of events, Laura covered her ears with her hands.

'Don't tell me any more,' she sighed. 'Just decide on a plan of action and we'll do it.'

Phoenix couldn't help but smile. There was a heart as true as steel inside Laura, and thank the stars for it.

'We've no time to spare,' he said. 'We can't wait any longer. We've got to do it now.'

All the while they were creeping forward towards the Gorgons' cave, the words of Pan were running through Phoenix's head.

The myth is a pole star to navigate your way.

And his second, more ominous piece of advice.

By the time the moon has crossed the sky thrice over.

Phoenix went through every detail he had ever read about the Perseus story and listed them mentally.

Medusa is my target. Pick the wrong Gorgon and I will be killed.

I mustn't look directly into her eyes. I can only look at her reflection in the shield.

When I sever the head I have to keep clear of Medusa's blood. It burns like the most powerful acid.

Then he came to one detail that chilled his blood. The helmet of invisibility would hide him from the Gorgons' stare. Except it wouldn't. It had gone. And all thanks to Adams.

He's no minor irritation, thought Phoenix. The game has him now. He is no longer just a small town bully, he really is my Nemesis.

Laura peered over a ridge.

'Is that it?'

'That's it.'

'But who are all those people?'

In the choking mist there were silhouettes of ten, maybe twenty still figures.

'All the adventurers who came looking for the Medusa.'

'But what are they doing?'

144

'Doing, Laura? They aren't doing anything. They're dead, victims of the Gorgon's stare.'

Laura's eyes narrowed.

'So they're—'

'Statues. People have come here many times to slay the demon, but every one of them has looked into her eyes and suffered the same fate. She turned them all to stone.'

Laura peered through the stinking fog. 'And we're going in *there*?'

'Like I told you; we've got no choice.'

Another click on his score bracelet. Five more points gone.

'See?'

'And if we don't complete our mission in time?'

'Then we lose,' Phoenix answered, 'or worse.'

He checked the sickle and slid his arm through the strap of the shield.

'Now stay close to me.'

His heart was pounding, but it was even worse for Laura. At the thought of what lay ahead, her legs were giving way under her. Her earlier determination was crumbling.

'Phoenix, I'm not sure I can go in there.'

'You must.'

'But why? This is your quest, not mine.'

He took a deep breath.

'I've told you, Laura, like it or not, you are part of this.'

'Phoenix, I just can't.'

He looked her straight in the eye and spoke to her as simply and directly as he could, 'Laura, you're not the only one who's afraid. I need you.'

She bit her lip and gave the briefest of nods. They started to move forward through the poisoned air.

'Here,' Phoenix whispered. 'Hold this over your face.' He passed her a piece of cloth.

'Where did this come from?'

'Let's just say my chiton is a bit shorter today.'

By now they had reached the forest of petrified souls.

Armed men caught in the moment of terror when they

looked into Medusa's eyes, sorceresses who had begun – but never finished – their spell to cast out the demon, even fantastic animals frozen to the spot where they came across the Gorgons. Over the years rain had worn away an arm here, part of a face there. But one thing remained in every one of the faces, the expression of utter horror at the sight of the foul sisters.

'Do you really think we have a chance?' Laura gasped, her voice coming out in snatches.

'Of course. I wouldn't be here otherwise.'

There, the words came easily. But would courage follow?

'Now, not another sound until we leave the cave with the Medusa's head. It could cost us our lives.'

Laura took him at his word. But her next attempt at communication almost dislocated Phoenix's shoulder. The thump to get his attention sent a stabbing pain through his arm and neck. Turning questioning – and wounded – eyes towards her, he was directed to movement around the mouth of the cave. The Gorgons.

'Sistersss, he is here.'

Instinctively, he flattened himself against the sodden, slimy earth. Laura followed suit.

'Hiding, boy? That won't help you. Sooner or later you must show yourself.'

He rolled on to his back and drew the sickle. Motioning with his head, he willed Laura to follow him through the mist.

'There!' came the voice of Medusa. 'I hear him. He is coming.'

Her sisters were sniffing the air. Like dogs. And excited as dogs. They were rearing, straining to catch sight of the hero.

'Yes, yes, it's true. He is coming. I can almost taste his flesh.'

Phoenix kept his gaze turned from Laura. The last thing he needed was to betray his growing terror. Keeping their step as light as they could on the spongy ground, they scurried between the Gorgons' petrified victims and cowered behind a boulder at the cave's mouth. They were to the left of the sisters and slightly behind them. While Phoenix struggled to control his breathing he became aware of Laura staring round, alerted to something behind them. He gave a questioning frown. She shrugged in return.

'Show yourself, boy.'

'What'sss the matter? Too frightened? Yes, that's it, isn't it? The skin is creeping off your bones, isn't it? You wish you were a babe again, in the safety of your mother's armsss.'

The other Gorgons took up the refrain. 'Mummy, mummy.'

'Did you know?' Medusa rasped. 'That's what the warrior does at his death. Yes, you heard me correctly, boy. As the big, bearded hero crawls through his own blood, he starts calling for his mother. Mummy! Mummy!'

Phoenix tried to shut out their sly, wheedling voices, but he couldn't help himself. He saw Mum's face. Danäe's too.

The sisters joined the chorus. 'Mummy! Mummy!'

Then a cackle of triumph.

'Let's get this over boy. What's one more childless mother in this world of pain?'

I don't need to listen to you, you twisted demons, thought Phoenix. I know your game. You want to plant the terror inside my head, to freeze my muscles and kill my courage. I can't let you. I mustn't.

But the noise was getting to Laura. She was still darting glances behind her.

For crying out loud, Laura, the danger's over there. Right in front of you.

He tapped her on the arm, almost scaring her out of her skin. Waiting a moment to let her steady her nerves, Phoenix pointed to a recess deeper inside the cave. She nodded. But as they scrambled over the slippery rocks he lost his footing and fell heavily.

'There,' Medusa declared triumphantly. 'I have him, sis-tersss.'

Phoenix shuddered at her snake-slithering approach and tightened his grip on the sickle.

She'll be upon me any second.

147

'Welcome boy, welcome to my home, your mausoleum.'

He twisted his head and looked into the shield. Her form towered over him, the movement of the snakes writhing its way inside his brain. He drew back his arm to strike but the blow never fell. Instead it felt as if somebody had hit him hard on his wrist. The sickle span across the cave's uneven, water-logged floor.

'Phoenix,' Laura cried, throwing caution to the winds. 'That's what I was trying to tell you. Somebody has been behind us all along, stalking us.'

Half paralysed with fear at Medusa's approach Phoenix found it hard to take in what Laura meant.

'Listen to me,' Laura continued. 'The helmet didn't just disappear. It was stolen. Somebody's using it against us. Here in the cave, we have an invisible enemy. And I think you know who.'

Phoenix felt the rush of air as Medusa lashed out with a bronze claw, and he threw himself out of her reach. Scrambling to his feet, he retreated to a shelf of rock.

'Of course,' he panted, 'Adams.'

'That's right,' came a voice, a boy's voice like his own, just beginning to break. 'Surprise surprise.'

'You again.'

But there was no time to dwell on his unwelcome arrival. The Gorgons were on the move, encircling Phoenix. In the corner of his eye he could see Laura crawling forward, reaching for the sickle. Just as she was closing her fingers around the handle, it skipped away as if it had a life of its own. Adams again. Phoenix could hear his footsteps, but how to find him? Backing away from the Gorgons, he found himself standing knee-deep in water.

That's it, that's how to see him!

Using the wallet, Phoenix scooped up a bucketful of the stagnant liquid and waited.

'This is a poor fight,' Medusa taunted. 'Can this really be the hero we were promised? The others put up a much better fight.'

Ignoring the words, Phoenix focused on Adams' footsteps. There! Without a moment's hesitation he flung the water and watched it splash off his invisible form. Hurling himself at Adams, Phoenix pinned him to the floor and wrenched off the helmet.

'I could kill you for this,' he yelled. 'I could kill you, Adams!'

But Adams wriggled free and made a dash for the cave. Attracted to the movement, all three Gorgons set off in pursuit.

'You all right, Laura?'

'I'm fine, but what about Steve?'

Phoenix pulled on the helmet.

'What about him?'

'I know what he's done, but you can't let them kill him.'

Why not? He'll only come back to haunt us.

'Phoenix,' Laura cried, as if reading his mind. 'He's sly and he's nasty. But look what's happening. They'll rip him to shreds. He doesn't deserve that. He isn't evil.'

Phoenix picked up the sickle.

'All right, I'll save him.'

Climbing to the highest point in the cave he shouted a challenge to the sisters.

'What's the matter? Picking on small fry?'

His heart was thudding in his chest. Either this was very brave, or very foolish.

The Gorgons span round and Phoenix took refuge in the shield's reflection. He could make out the approach of their monstrous forms. Satisfied that Adams had made his getaway, Phoenix prepared for battle. He recalled what he'd seen in Deicterion and etched every detail of the Gorgon, Medusa in his mind.

He had to choose the right sister. But as he readied himself for the fight, his heart turned to ice.

Outside the cave the light was fading, replaced by dense, moonless night.

'Phoenix,' cried Laura, realizing their predicament. 'It's nightfall.'

How would they ever recognize Medusa in the dark?

6

The nightmare had returned. Phoenix thought he'd been scared before, but this! Every moment filled him with hopeless, gut-melting horror. It was like being back in the labyrinth, dragging his fear through the darkness. Every sound seemed closer. He could make out the slide of the Gorgons on the waterlogged bottom of the cave, the hiss of their serpent-wreathed hair, their taunting shrieks.

'No escape now, boy. Don't think the helmet of invisibility will save you. We can smell you, boy. We can smell your fear.'

'No way out,' the second Gorgon told him. 'Do you know your fate, boy? Your dying will not be quick. First we will destroy your mind, then we will devour the rest of you. Do you know what we've got in store? It's not the forest of statues for you. No, we've a special treat. First, you will hear us feed on the heart of the girl, then we will come for you.'

I know what you're after, thought Phoenix. You want me to call out to Laura, to give away my position. But I'm not falling for it. Hear me, you monsters? I won't do it.

'Show yourself, hero, you know that time is running out.'

Phoenix glanced at the points display. Only fifty points left. Time was indeed running out. He peered into the gloom. One of the Gorgons had installed herself at the mouth of the cave to prevent their escape. He could make her out quite clearly. But what about the others? They were moving unseen through the deeper dark of the interior. They could be anywhere. He heard movement to his right. The Gorgons? And what if it was Adams? What if he'd come back to finish the job? Phoenix felt

151

the bracelet click again. Forty-five points left. Time had almost run out. The task was enormous. He felt the hero in him detaching itself. His power to think and act was being stripped from him. He couldn't go on.

And if we lose, what do we lose?

Maybe it would be better to throw down his weapon and show himself.

He was desolate. All he wanted to do was surrender to the Gorgon's stare.

Do we just lose the game, or our lives as well?

No, he thought, his mind rejecting his cowardice. I can't just sit here. Got to fight. He edged towards the noise, raising the sickle ready to strike. As he reached out, he heard a yelp of panic. Thank goodness, it's Laura.

Got to reassure her. 'Shh. It's me.'

'Phoenix! What do we do now?'

But his mind was blank. Laura was unarmed. What *could* she do? Then his thoughts were interrupted by the voice of Medusa.

'Come sister, he is here. I smell him. Yes, I smell his fear, the sickness, the sourness of it.'

Phoenix could just about distinguish two hideous shapes. But which was Medusa? He found himself backing deeper into the cave. Laura was moving too, retreating at his pace. His thoughts were racing.

How do I tell one sister from another? How?

Forty points left.

'Can this be the hero?' came Medusa's voice. 'This wretched boy cowering in the dark? Surely not.'

Unnatural laughter filled the cave, echoing into the depths of Phoenix's soul.

'Listen to him, sister. The coward can hardly breathe.' Then the thin, insinuating voice was replaced by a deafening roar. 'SHOW YOURSELF!'

'SHOW YOURSELF!'

'SHOW!'

The echo boomed around the walls of the cave, the

vibrations quivering inside his skin. There was no escape. The display clicked to thirty-five.

'Time's almost out.'

'Phoenix, we have to do something.'

But fear had him by the throat. He could only think of one thing. Escape. An end to the terror.

'Where are you, little hero?' called the sisters. 'Scary in the dark isn't it? You never know what's next to you?'

'They're right,' Phoenix panted. 'We need some light.'

'Light,' said Laura excitedly. 'But we've got light. The flare Pan gave me.'

'What's that? What's she saying sistersss?'

'Light, what does the girl mean?'

The Gorgons were worried. For the first time doubt crept into their voices.

'Laura,' Phoenix whispered, 'you must be onto something. They're scared.'

Terror was beginning to relax its grip.

'When I give the order,' he told her. 'Set off the flare and cover your eyes.'

Their score was down to thirty.

He braced himself, measuring the distance to the two looming shapes in the darkness. Turning his back, Phoenix looked down at the polished surface of the shield.

'Now!'

The intense light of the flare exploded into the cave, sending stabbing pains through his eyes. For a moment he was utterly blinded, then he turned to look at the shield. He could see them, the Gorgons.

Is that her?

Shorter than her sisters, her tongue protruding more grotesquely, the writhing pattern of snakes denser and more revolting.

Is that her?

The score hit twenty-five.

'Phoenix, what are you waiting for?'

Yes, that's her. It's got to be. Strike. Do it now.

153

The bracelet began to flash. Twenty. Fifteen.

Scurrying sideways like a crab, Phoenix kept his neck twisted and his head turned away from those terrible eyes. He looked into the burnished shield. Pausing only to squash one last doubt he swung the sickle.

The score glowed ominously. Ten points.

With a cry, Phoenix struck an upward blow, putting every ounce of fear and anger into the thrust – fear and anger *and courage*.

A shriek of pain crashed round the cave, as pitiful as it was hideous, the death throes of Medusa.

Five points.

Again, strike again.

Measuring his blow, Phoenix sliced through flesh, muscle, bone. He beheaded the Gorgon. But in doing so he unleashed a scalding torent of tarry, venomous blood. The points bracelet was racing, the vibration fairly drilling into his wrist.

'Laura. Get back.'

They hurled themselves out of the way of the blood-venom and watched fascinated as it burned through the stone floor of the cave.

'Is it safe?'

'I think so. Only one way to find out.'

Reaching for the severed head he felt the twist of the snakes over his wrist. Forcing down the temptation to be sick, he bundled the head into the wallet.

His score was still mounting.

'Laura, let's go.'

But the battle wasn't over. Laura was screaming.

'Behind you!'

Phoenix felt the beat of wings, the grief-stricken snarl. One of Medusa's sisters was mounting her own attack.

'Laura, my hand. Grab it. Now!'

The sandals took them into the air just as the Gorgon's claw shattered the boulder in front of them. The force of the blow sent them spinning, and knocked the helmet clean off Phoenix's head. For the second time he had no disguise.

154

'Don't let go. Whatever you do, Laura, hold tight.'

'Phoenix, the third Gorgon. Where is she?'

He could see the second sister sliding after them, too far away to pose a danger. But the third? She'd left her place at the mouth of the cave. Why?

'Look!'

The stagnant water beneath them was beginning to boil. Suddenly, the Gorgon's head erupted through the floor sending rocks hurtling across the cave. Her face loomed violently in front of them.

'Shut your eyes, Laura. Whatever you do, don't look.'

Locking his eyes on the shield's reflection, Phoenix searched for the cavemouth and escape.

The way out. I don't see it. I DON'T SEE IT.

He was tempted to turn his head. The Gorgon was reading his mind.

'That's it, boy, turn. You want the way out? Well, let me help you. This way. You just have to look this way.'

But the Gorgons didn't wait for him to turn. They gathered over their dead sister, then mounted their attack, rising on their serpent tails and snapping with their jaws. The sound was deafening, like iron doors slamming over and over again. Soon Laura's cries and Phoenix's own added to the din in the cave.

We'll never get out!

The closest of the sisters coiled herself then hurled her grotesque frame upward in a determined assault. A sharpened tusk sliced through the skin on Phoenix's shoulder.

'Hunh!'

By hurling himself backwards Phoenix managed to prevent serious damage, but the pain was burning all down one side. He remembered Dad's wound in the castle of Procrustes. If he still harboured any doubts, the attack ended them. The game was real all right.

We're finished.

Phoenix was struggling to avoid the second of the Gorgons when he glimpsed a silvery glow.

Of course. The moon. Ready to cross the sky for the third time.

'Laura,' he cried. 'The moon. Look at it. The moon is up.'

There was no more time for delay. Seizing the moment, they swooped out into the chill of the night. Their score was back in the thousands and mounting rapidly. They skipped over the moonlit clouds.

Victorious!

They were back over Deicterion when Phoenix began his descent.

'Phoenix, what are you doing?'

'There's something I have to see.'

'But what about those streetfighters? Why put ourselves in danger again?'

She gestured at the bloodstained cloth on his arm.

'Especially with that wound.'

Phoenix pointed to the carving of the Gorgons.

'Because of that.'

He led her to the giant representation.

'It's Medusa,' she said. 'But we don't need the carving any more. Why—'

'Look,' Phoenix told her. 'At the base. It didn't mean anything last time.'

There was a number. A *score*. Five thousand.

'Check the display,' Laura said excitedly.

'5005,' Phoenix read. 'But what's the winning score?'

He found himself wandering along the alley that skirted the city wall. Laura moved ahead of him.

'Phoenix,' she said suddenly. 'Come here.'

Another carving, as massive as that of the Gorgons. This time it pictured the Minotaur.

'But there's no score.'

'There is here,' said Laura.

In the corner of the carving there was a small detail. The door to the labyrinth, and below it the number 7000.

'Seven thousand!' Phoenix cried. '*Seven* thousand to enter

the labyrinth. But what else have we got to do? How do we score that? We're 2000 short of our target.'

'Here's your answer,' Laura announced, walking further along the wall.

Phoenix reached her side and ran his fingers over the numbers. Two thousand. Then he traced the lines of a familiar face. The tyrant-king of Seriphos.

'Of course,' Phoenix sighed, remembering the myth. 'Another has to die. Polydectes.'

7

Back in John Graves' study, Phoenix's mother was laughing hysterically, great blobs of tears spilling over her cheeks and dropping from her chin. She wanted to run to somebody, hug them, tell them that her boy was all right. But there was nobody to tell. They were all mummified, entombed in a single, unchanging instant of time. For once the voice in the computer had no words to commemorate Medusa's death. Instead, as if to mourn her passing, the screen images blurred and the sequences of numbers raced more madly than ever, throbbing and pulsating until Mum had to shield her eyes.

'Don't go wrong now,' she cried as she lost sight of Phoenix.

There was a flash and every clock in the house started ticking simultaneously. Time had started again. Mum hadn't noticed. She was trying to make the computer work.

But the flash wasn't a technical fault.

It was a cry of despair.

Inside the computer, something was screaming.

There were no black flags over the tyrant's palace this time. As Phoenix and Laura approached Polydectes' citadel, there was gaiety in the air. Red banners vied with yellow, snapping in the strong sea breeze. They dropped to earth in the cover of an olive grove.

'Are you sure you're ready for this?' asked Laura.

'My arm, you mean? It's fine. A bit stiff, and that's easing.'

He weighed the Gorgon's head in the leather wallet.

'You know what we have to do?'

158

He saw Laura's downcast eyes and felt some sympathy. Killing a man in cold blood is hard.

'We're so close to completing our mission. We have to do it.'

'But it's so calculated. To turn a man to stone. And without giving him a chance.'

'It's no more than we did to Medusa.'

Laura showed signs of frustration. 'She was a monster.'

'And so is Polydectes.'

'Maybe,' said Laura. 'But even if he is, he's a human one.' She rested a hand on his arm. 'What's he done that's so terrible? He wants to marry Danaë. Hardly a capital offence. And OK, he set you up, but it's all part of the game. Adams has done worse, but we didn't try to kill him. Let's face it, Phoenix. How do we know he's a tyrant? Because the legend says so. How do we know we have to destroy him? Because the game says so. Everything is because the game says so.'

Phoenix continued to cling stubbornly to his plan of action.

'That's enough for me.'

'Well, not for me. You've said it yourself. The game is cruel. You can't trust it.'

'Don't you think I know that?'

They faced each other, angry and tense.

'Ask yourself one simple question, Laura. Do you want to stay here forever? Do you?'

'Of course not. It doesn't mean we have to do this. It's wrong.'

Giving a snort of exasperation, Phoenix stormed off to the cliff's edge. He felt the wind on his face and he knew he was right.

Polydectes must die!

He span round. 'Why can't you understand? You're not home in Brownleigh now. Mum and Dad aren't there to sort it out. You can't phone 999. Normal rules don't apply here. You learn the ways of the game or you perish.'

'What makes you so right all the time?' Laura retorted. 'You're not infallible. I was the one who knew there was somebody in the cave, not you. I thought of the flare, not you.

And there was the arrow. I pulled you back then, too. I've saved your life more than once, remember. What makes you think you know everything?'

'All right,' Phoenix yelled back. 'I'm human. I make mistakes. But I'm the only one who can get us home. I'm the Legendeer. Don't try to stop me, Laura. Polydectes must die.'

Laura turned away. There was no bridging the gulf between them.

'Do what you have to.'

'Here,' Phoenix snarled, tossing the shield and the sickle to the ground. 'I'm leaving these with you.' He slipped off the sandals and threw them to Laura. Finally he hoisted the head of Medusa on to his shoulders. 'You could still come with me.'

'No,' said Laura, her back still turned to him. 'Not this time.'

Without another word, Phoenix set off for the palace with his gruesome wedding gift. By the time he had reached the outer battlements the marriage feast was beginning. He heard the blare of trumpets and the beat of drums. Flower petals were being showered on the arriving guests. He looked up at the maids emptying baskets of petals over the crowds and scowled.

I am coming, Polydectes.

He was at the doors to the great hall before he was challenged.

'Young Perseus, eh?' said the guard. 'I didn't expect to see you again.'

'I return to give Lord Polydectes his wedding present.'

He raised the leather wallet.

'Then you'd better go inside, though Olympus knows what King Polydectes will make of it. He thinks you're on a quest for Medusa's head. I ask you, a boy sent to slay the demon.'

Phoenix smiled.

'You know me and my idle boasts.'

The guard smiled back.

'I do that. In you go, lad.'

The hall was full of Polydectes' guards and hangers-on. Of all

160

the people in the hall, only Danaë was innocent. Phoenix made his way to her side.

'Lady Danaë,' he whispered. 'When I begin to speak, avert your eyes.'

She stared at the wallet.

'You mean—'

'Yes, I succeeded in my quest.'

She slipped away from the table without a word and retired to a recess where silken curtains hung. Satisfied that she was safely out of the way, Phoenix strode towards King Polydectes' throne.

'Polydectes,' he declared, 'I return with the Gorgon's head.'

Polydectes turned, and all his guests with him.

'You dare walk back into my court?' he cried, baring his wolf's teeth. 'And with some tall tale about bringing the Gorgon's head. You'd better be a good runner, boy, because my guards will chase you all the way back to the end of the world, or wherever you've been hiding yourself.'

Laughter rippled through the crowded hall.

'But it's true,' Phoenix insisted. 'I have the head.'

More mocking laughter.

'Lords and ladies of Seriphos,' Phoenix shouted. 'Invited guests. You have a choice before you. I swear that I have here the head of the Gorgon, Medusa. King Polydectes seems to doubt me. Let's have a game. All those who believe the king, stand with him. All who trust me, stand at my side.'

There was raucous laughter from the guests as they moved over towards Polydectes.

Phoenix's side of the hall emptied steadily until he stood alone.

'There you are, boy,' boasted Polydectes. 'That's how many believe in the boy-hero. Do your worst *hero*.'

Phoenix did as he was told. He reached into the wallet and produced the head of Medusa. He watched with satisfaction as horror registered in the eyes of every one of Polydectes' court. In the time it took to blink an eye, a fantastic transformation had taken place. Skin that was tanned and soft turned as

161

wrinkled as an elephant's hide. As hard as granite. Where there had been a hundred laughing guests, a hundred stone statues now stood.

Phoenix was returning the head to the wallet, smiling grimly at his growing points score, when Danaë emerged from the recess.

'Lady,' he told her. 'You are free.'

She took his hand, but not to thank him.

'Listen,' she said urgently. 'I may only have minutes.'

She lifted her hair to display an owl tattoo.

'That's right. I could die on the spot for talking to you. But too many lives hang in the balance. I wish I could have found the courage earlier. I have to say my piece, whatever the cost. Enough of this play-acting. Nobody can be free until the Gamesmaster is destroyed. Even if you kill the Minotaur, you won't have won. Know this, Legendeer. The labyrinth is not the end.'

'How can you be sure? How do you know about the Minotaur? How do you know? You're—'

'There's no time for that. Listen to me, and listen well.'

She leaned forward and whispered in Phoenix's ear. 'Only one man knows how to win the game. Find him and you will free us all.'

'But who?'

There was a sudden, sickening thump in Danaë's throat. Her lovely pale eyes rolled back and her breath rattled in her throat. The soft, reassuring voice was drowning in blood.

'No!' cried Phoenix.

He cradled the dying woman.

'Please. Don't die.'

She smiled, blood staining her gasping lips.

'Too late. But the man who can beat the game. It's your father.'

Then came a desperate struggle for breath, before the moment of dark crisis came, and she died.

Don't die. Don't leave me.

Phoenix slumped to his knees. He was alone and crushed by

162

Danaë's death. Phoenix was still taking in what Danaë had told him, wondering about the identity of the Gamesmaster, when he heard the palace guard arriving at the run.

'Treason!' they cried. 'Treachery against the king.'

In fury at the death of Danaë, Phoenix showed them the head and they cried no more. Ten more statues had joined the hundred in the hall.

'Laura,' he called, reaching the path that led down to the beach. 'I'm back. It's over.'

There was no reply.

'Laura,' he shouted again.

His heart began to race.

Why doesn't she reply?

He started to run.

'Laura!'

As he reached the sands his worst fears were confirmed. Written on the beach in letters three feet high was a chilling message:

SURPRISE SURPRISE.

THE LEVELS

Level Ten
Into the Labyrinth

1

'Laura!'

Phoenix had scoured the barren beaches of Seriphos for hours, but there was no sign of her. He even staggered into the waves, beating the water with his fists. All to no avail. He was no hero now, just a boy alone. It was even worse than that. Now that he'd known real friendship, the loss of it weighed even more heavily. It was as if part of him had been ripped out and his whole body was outraged by the gaping, throbbing wound. He sank to his knees by the message written in the sand

SURPRISE SURPRISE.

I could kill you, Adams.

This time Phoenix really meant it. Wherever there was danger, wherever there was evil, Adams was there to give it a helping hand. Beyond the screen, in a backwater like Brownleigh, he had been a small town bully. Here, under the influence of the game, he was deadly. He was Reede's disciple. Dad might hold the key to the game, but, like Laura, he was a minor player.

It's a two-player game, Adams, and it is between us.

*You **are** my Nemesis.*

A terrible thought struck him.

'And it's all my fault. I invited you in!'

When Adams entered the game he started drinking from evil's cup. There was no doubt any more, he had become intoxicated with the taste. That was it. The two boys were enemies to the last beat of their hearts, the last breath in their bodies.

More than just a game? Adams, you don't know how much more!

Phoenix patted the wallet containing Medusa's head. Kill him. Maybe he should.

He dug his fingers into the silvery sand and felt utterly broken and defeated. He was as sorry for himself as he'd ever felt in his life. He wanted to curse the gods, or Reede, or whoever was making this crazy world turn, but he wasn't going to give them the satisfaction of hearing his misery echoing over the booming tide. They thought they were so clever with their game, didn't they? They had their hero, somebody to put through every trial. Now they had their villain too, to track him all the way. Adams and I, Phoenix thought, we're two sides of the coin, adversaries in a lethal game.

He thought of Danaë dying and Laura kidnapped. Every ounce of his growing confidence had evaporated.

I can't stand it any more. It has to end. It's all too much. I want out.

But how *could* he escape? And how could he leave without Dad and Laura? It was only then, as he abandoned hope of ever finding her on the island, that he gave the beach a proper investigation. What he had missed before now became obvious. It was the footprints. His own, of course. Then Laura's. A set for Adams. Then there was the imprint of a pair of cloven hooves.

Pan.

Laura had been right about him all along. At best he was an unreliable guide, at worst— He didn't like to think about it. Phoenix sat watching the tide roll in, wondering what to do next. He was beginning to realize how great a setback he had suffered. It wasn't just Laura he had lost. The flying sandals were gone, the helmet, shield and sickle. Every single thing that told him he'd made progress in the game. But it couldn't end here.

I won, didn't I?

So why hadn't he moved on to the next level? Why was he still stranded on Seriphos? He checked the points display. There! All seven thousand points. His sense of injustice boiled over. He had to face the Minotaur one last time. He had to destroy the creature that haunted his dreams.

But how?

He was at his lowest ebb, staring at the writing in the sand and feeling his loss like pain, when he heard something, a high, piercing screech. High above, swooping from the cloudless sky came a great bird. Like an eagle, but even bigger, with a wing span at least twice as wide. The bird was tracing vast circles in the sky. Phoenix watched fascinated as it glided closer, a huge predator with the most brilliant plumage he'd ever seen – blue, purple, scarlet and gold.

'The phoenix! You're the phoenix aren't you, my namesake. The bird who rises from the ashes.'

He watched spellbound as the great bird swooped over the sands. Phoenix raced after it, on and on, round the rocky headland towards a stretch of beach he hadn't seen, never mind explored. As he staggered exhausted around a screen of rocks, he cried out. On the beach, the phoenix had built a funeral pyre. Phoenix watched as his namesake bound together the ingredients of the pyre: aromatic plants, incense and balsam, threaded into a nest of twigs and branches. He breathed in the scent, mysterious yet familiar, the mingled odour of life and death. He was becoming drowsy, exhausted by the events of the last few days.

He re-ran them all in his mind: the fight at Deicterion, the beheading of Medusa, his revenge against Polydectes, and now Laura's kidnap. He was slipping into a hazy dreamstate, half waking, half sleeping.

167

Playing the game . . .

. . . the stench of the underground prison . . .

. . . its endless passageways . . .

. . . THE ROAR OF THE BEAST!

Phoenix was shocked awake. The nightmare had returned. But he didn't feel horror – he felt hope. Propping himself up on one elbow, he began to focus on the scene before him. The fire of life and death was scorching the sands. Smoke was billowing into the sky, roaring flames dancing at the water's edge, burning with such fury that the tidewaters boiled. And there at its heart was the great bird, beating its wings in the red and orange of the fire. He could feel the flames licking around him, but he didn't burn. It was a gentle, healing fire. As he looked through the acrid smoke he saw a familiar figure, come to witness the event.

Pan was standing at the water's edge, silent and watching.

Now Phoenix understood. The bird's death was his rebirth. There was more than evil at work in this legend world. There was good too, and it was working through him. As the bird's dying screech filled the sky Phoenix saw his arms fading, becoming transparent.

Through the woodsmoke Pan gave a brief, cryptic nod, as if formally witnessing the Legendeer's progress, then strode away into the surf.

At last! Phoenix was moving to the next level.

2

Another quest, another forest of black flags snapping in the sea breeze. Phoenix shook his head. Death hung over the game like a cloud.

'Hey! HEY!' Phoenix shouted to a passing street urchin. 'Where am I?'

The boy scratched his head. 'Are you serious?'

'I just want to know where I am.'

'Look around you,' he said. 'What do you see? Only the greatest city in all Greece, beloved of Pallas Athene, sorrowing Athens itself.'

Though he was sure from the moment he stepped on to the street exactly how the boy would answer, Phoenix still needed to hear it from his lips.

'Why sorrowing?'

'Where have you been, stranger? Because King Minos demands his tribute, that's why. This year, as every year, seven youths and seven maidens will be transported to the palace of Knossos on a black-sailed death ship. Every well-born family in this city has lost a son or a daughter. There in the palace of merciless King Minos, the razer of cities, they will be thrown to the beast that dwells in the labyrinth.'

Phoenix breathed deeply. Now he knew why the nightmare had begun again. He had almost come full circle, to resume his mission where he had broken off and fled in terror.

Where I begged for my life.

He felt his cowardice keenly. He had abandoned Dad, left him to his fate. There was only one way to make amends. He had to be the hero he claimed to be, the Legendeer. He'd played Perseus to the end, and played his part bravely.

He'd conquered the Gorgon, Medusa and destroyed Polydectes. There was only one way to make amends, he had to win the game.

'Which way to the royal palace?' he asked.

But the boy was staring past him, eyes widening. Phoenix turned and saw what he was looking at.

'Pan.'

He strode to the shadowy recess where his guide was waiting.

'Another of my tricks, Legendeer?'

Phoenix didn't reply. Instead, he watched as his guide's nose swelled into a monstrous snout and his head sprouted horns.

The Minotaur.

Returning to his normal state, Pan spoke, but without the gaiety he had displayed in his earlier appearances.

Can it be?

You are actually beginning to fear me?

'Welcome to the next stage of your journey.'

Phoenix returned Pan's gaze coldly. He remembered the prints on the beach. He was in the presence of a treacherous god.

'Where's Laura?'

'She's for you to find,' Pan replied without a trace of emotion in his voice. 'It was your carelessness that left the girl prey to the fates.'

'Me!' cried Phoenix. 'You dare to blame me. Why—'

Pan waved away his furious protests.

'I am sure you have worked out where you are,' he said. 'And who.'

He eyed the wallet carrying Medusa's head and stroked it lightly.

'You won't be needing that here, Legendeer. It is time for the hero to take on a new form. Hail to thee, Theseus, heir to the throne of Athens.'

Phoenix was about to pepper Pan with questions when he

170

was cut off by the sound of a procession. Drums beat and trumpets blared.

'The king?' he asked.

There was no reply. Pan had gone. Phoenix found himself standing in the front row of a growing crowd, drawn by the approach of the royal party. But there was no cheering, no applause. The mood was sombre. Every building flew a black flag. After a few moments, he discovered the boy he had spoken to before Pan's appearance.

'What are you?' the boy asked, glancing back at the recess. 'A god?'

'No,' said Phoenix with a smile. 'Not a god.'

The boy didn't seem reassured by his answer.

'The death ship,' Phoenix asked, 'when does it sail?'

'Tomorrow, at dawn.'

There was no time to lose. Phoenix remembered the words of Pan. *Use the myth as a pole star to navigate your way*. He turned the legend over in his mind. King Aegeus of Athens fathers Theseus in a distant town called Troezen, but doesn't stay to see him born. He leaves the boy a sword and a pair of sandals hidden under a great rock to remember him by. When Theseus is approaching manhood, he rolls back the stone and discovers the secret of his birth.

Remembering the way Pan had stroked the leather wallet containing Medusa's head, Phoenix felt inside. In place of the gory trophy he discovered the hilt of a broken sword and an ancient pair of sandals.

Phoenix looked at them. The belongings of Aegeus that had lain concealed under the boulder in Troezen.

My destiny.

If I'm to win the game I must claim my destiny.

An advance party of soldiers was marching into the square, carrying black flags. 'Make way for King Aegeus and Queen Medea.'

Phoenix then stared at the king, aging and bowed. There was nothing for it. He had to make himself known. If he could slay the Gorgon, he could speak to the king. He stepped forward and immediately drew the attention of three of the king's bodyguards.

'Wait,' Phoenix cried as they converged on him, swords drawn. 'I wish to petition the king.'

The soldiers glanced round at Aegeus.

'Let the boy speak.'

'My name,' he announced, 'is Theseus.'

A murmur ran through the crowd. The king leaned forward, examining every inch of Phoenix's face.

'I come from Troezen to claim my birthright as your son and heir to the throne of Athens.'

He saw the eyes of the king's wife, Queen Medea burning into him. Those eyes, he'd seen them before . . . somewhere . . . Thrown by the piercing stare of the queen, Phoenix struggled on. But even as he spoke, he was unsettled by those scintillating, black diamond eyes.

'I have travelled many days and many nights to reach your court.'

'Your coming has been announced,' said Aegeus. 'The Oracle spoke of the boy-hero and his deeds. We have been waiting for your arrival.'

Phoenix knew exactly what to say. None of his reading had been wasted. Time to draw on it now. He recalled his and Dad's first attempts at this level.

'I came by the coast road, a bandit-ridden place. I defeated Periphetes the cudgel man, Procrustes with his magic bed and Sinis who ties his victims to trees. I destroyed a wild sow and the thief Scirion.'

In truth, Dad had done all that, but the tale came to his lips as easily as treachery to those of Adams. They were both becoming skilled in the ways of the game.

'Finally, I mastered Cercyon the Arcadian and Polyphemon, butcher of travellers.'

'Great adventures indeed,' said Aegeus. 'And travellers will long sing your name. May the reputation of great Theseus echo down the hallways of time. But what is your mission?'

Before Phoenix could answer, Medea began to speak.

'Welcome, bold Theseus. This mean street is no place to greet a hero. Come to the palace this evening. We will prepare a banquet in your honour.'

Her words were welcoming but her scheming eyes blazed with hatred. He could feel her power like an electrical charge in the air.

'We will speak further then of your adventures and your claim to the throne.'

Aegeus clapped his hands.

'Guards, conduct our visitor to his chambers and make him comfortable. We will see you tonight, bandit slayer.'

It was as he passed Medea that Phoenix caught the glare of her eyes again. Now he knew where he had seen them before. It was there, in the labyrinth, among the blood and the splintered bones. It was *her* eyes he'd seen staring down at him through the bars of the grating.

3

Two hours later Phoenix was standing at the window of his room, watching darkness fall over Athens. The death ship sailed the next day, and he had to be on board. Somewhere, the game had Dad and Laura. Phoenix remembered all the cruel things he had said to Dad, and the night filled with regret. But remorse wasn't going to solve anything. If any of them were ever to get out of this nightmare, he had to reach the labyrinth. He stared out across the paved square where huge braziers were burning, tossing showers of sparks into the twilit sky. Along the broad avenue that led to the palace, great black flags billowed in the strong sea breeze. A breeze that blew all the way to Crete and the lair of the beast. It could probably smell his fear already.

Suddenly, Phoenix froze. The hinges of the door to the chamber were creaking. Continuing to stand at the window, he felt on the table next to him for a weapon. His fingers came into contact with a large plate. The creaking had stopped, but muffled footsteps were approaching across the floor.

Just a little closer.

Half turning, Phoenix glimpsed a raised hand and a glinting dagger. Spinning round and kicking out his right leg, he tripped his assailant.

'Adams.'

In a reversal of their fortunes back home, Phoenix was sitting astride Adams, pinning his shoulders. No headaches now, he thought. Not one since I entered the game. For all the horror, I've never felt so alive. He tossed away the plate and recovered the dagger that had spun from Adams' hand.

174

'What are you doing here?'

Adams struggled in vain to get up.

'Playing my part,' he said, accepting defeat and lying back. 'I am Prince Medus, son of Medea and Aegeus. Your rival.'

My rival. What else?

'I should kill you right here,' snarled Phoenix.

Adams didn't show a grain of regret. No fear, either. In fact, he was as arrogant as if he were the one sitting astride Phoenix.

'What, and sign poor Laura's death warrant?'

A lump came to Phoenix's throat.

'Laura's here?'

'Let me up and I'll tell all.'

Reluctantly, Phoenix released his arch enemy. Adams didn't seem to mind being overcome so easily. That alone made Phoenix cautious.

'Tell me.'

Adams led him to the window and the black flags rippling against the stars.

'Those flags. They're for Laura.'

'You mean—'

'When the death ship sails tomorrow, she will be on board. But don't fret. You'll be seeing her tonight.'

'At the feast, you mean? How?'

Adams reclined on a couch, munching grapes. 'Tell me what you remember of the Theseus story.'

'I'm not going to—'

'Just tell the story, Legendeer. Remember, the myths are your guide.'

Back to that again. Telling stories of gods and demons. But that was his role. Adams was right; he was Phoenix, the Legendeer. He started the telling.

'King Minos is the ruler of Crete. Many years ago his son Androgeus visited Athens, but he was murdered in this very city. In revenge Minos waged war until a tribute was agreed. Every year seven youths and seven maidens are loaded onto a death ship and taken to the city of Knossos in his kingdom.

There they are fed to the Minotaur. The bones of his victims litter the floor of his maze. How am I doing?'

'You have the story to a tee,' said Adams. 'But I expected nothing less. That is exactly how King Aegeus told it to me. Here's the first bit of news. Laura has been chosen as one of those maidens. She'll be shown off with the others tonight.'

'This had better be the truth,' Phoenix warned.

'Oh, it is,' continued Adams. 'Now carry on with the story.'

'King Aegeus, Theseus' father, rules Athens, a city burdened by the terrible tribute. He marries twice, but there is no heir to the throne. Medea, his third wife, is a sorceress. She bears him the son he has craved, Medus—'

Adams stood up and took a bow.

'Yours truly. I'm the witch queen's son.'

Adams was barely recognizable as the small town bully he had once been. The game had transformed him. Such was the power of evil. But it had transformed Phoenix too.

Am I better, he wondered, or simply stronger? As he watched Adams, Phoenix saw a pattern. His enemy was part of a magical trinity of evil. Variations on a single monstrous name.

Medusa . . . Medea . . . Medus.

Of all the many heads of evil, these three loomed the largest in Phoenix's imagination. Medusa the Gorgon dies, Medea the sorceress rises in her place. Finally, waiting to ascend the throne, there is Medus. As the sorcerer-prince, Adams was now locked into the game. Evil would continue in an uninterrupted line.

'You can't win, you know,' Adams said smirking. 'Think about it. If old Aegeus declares you his heir, then the Queen's son remains second in line. And believe me, Medea isn't the kind of woman to accept second best.' He strode towards the door. 'Enjoy your meal.'

Phoenix watched Adams go and sat turning the warning over in his mind. He was taking it seriously. Anything that was in the legend was part of his destiny. At the banquet tonight, the Queen would try to poison Theseus. He thought of the

176

witch-queen and her hate-filled eyes. Yes, she planned to kill him.

As Adams' footfalls faded down the corridor, Phoenix inspected the contents of the leather wallet. The hilt of the sword was beautiful, twin serpents delicately carved into the ivory. Along with the sandals, it was his safeguard. The moment King Aegeus recognized them, he would accept him as his son. Then on to the labyrinth and the Minotaur, the key to finding his real father. Phoenix shouldered the wallet and waited to be fetched. The banquet would be another test.

He was in the tunnels again, running through the gloom. The beast was on his heels. He saw a sword on the floor and reached for it. But as he picked it up, it came to life in his hand. A snake, many snakes! They were twisting, slithering up his arm. This was no sword. He was holding the head of Medusa.

'No!'

He shook loose the chains of sleep, and sat up. There was a sheen of cold sweat on his skin. Would the nightmare never let him go?

A knock on the door swept away the last dusty cobwebs of drowsiness.

'Theseus, Prince of Athens. You are summoned to the palace.'

He followed the guard through the palace gardens and into the great hall. He remembered Polydectes and smiled at the thought of his silent, petrified court.

'Welcome, young Theseus,' said Aegeus. 'Take a seat at our table.'

Phoenix ran his eyes over the guests and stopped at a teenage boy watching him with malice-filled eyes. Adams.

'Ah,' said Aegeus, registering Phoenix's interest. 'This is my son Medus.'

Phoenix exchanged nods with Adams then gave the woman beside him a wary glance. The witch-queen, Medea.

'Before we eat,' said Aegeus. 'I have a sad duty.'

He raised a hand and the palace guards ushered in the

fourteen Athenians who were to die at the hands of the Minotaur. Laura was the third in the group.

'Youth of Athens,' Aegeus proclaimed. 'It is with a heavy heart that I salute you. Once in a twelvemonth, I bid farewell to the flower of this city as they lay down their sweet lives in the slaughterhouse of cruel King Minos. Be brave, my children. You surrender your fine young lives so that the citizens of Athens may sleep easy in their beds, free of war and dreadful slaughter.'

The fourteen stood in a line, facing the guests. There was fear in their faces.

'Now, Theseus, you have a tale to tell.'

'I do, King and father. I—'

'Before you continue,' Aegeus interrupted. 'A toast to the courage that brought you to my court.'

Phoenix saw Medea lean over to the king. Phoenix felt a twitch of foreboding. A maidservant charged his goblet. Medea whispered in her husband's ear. Adams watched the exchange between king and queen and smiled. Phoenix knew what they had in store for him.

'Hail to you, great Theseus,' cried Aegeus. 'A toast. To the slayer of bandits. Theseus of Troezen.'

Phoenix's heart kicked. The wine. Was this the poison? He stared at Laura and mouthed the word.

Poison.

For a moment her face wore a puzzled frown, then she understood. Yes, poison for the hero.

'Hail to you, great Aegeus,' Phoenix cried, raising the goblet.

He hesitated.

'Drink, brave Theseus,' said Adams. 'This banquet is in your honour.'

'Yes,' Medea added. 'Down your cup.'

Another glance at Laura. What did he do now?

'King Aegeus,' she said suddenly. 'May I speak?'

Surprised, Aegeus gave his consent. 'Tomorrow, you will make the greatest sacrifice for your city. You have leave to speak.'

178

All eyes turned towards Laura. It was Phoenix's chance. Leaning forward he tipped the goblet over and watched as the wine ran off the table. Adams was watching too. Just as he was about to call for more wine, Phoenix reached for the jug from which he filled his own cup.

'This will do fine,' he said with a smile.

Laura was stumbling through a feeble speech of praise for Aegeus, but it had done the trick. The wine, with its lacing of poison, was running through a crack in the tiled floor.

'Before I drink this toast,' Phoenix said, smiling triumphantly at Adams. 'Let me show you the proof that I am heir to the throne of Athens.'

But when he reached into the leather wallet his face drained of blood. The trinity of evil: Medusa, Medea, Medus. Instead of the sword hilt and the sandals, he felt the serpent hair of Medusa! The score bracelet registered the danger facing him. He was losing points.

'What is it, Theseus?' asked Medea, a smug satisfaction showing on her face.

'Is something wrong?' asked Adams.

Their voices were gloating. At the very moment when Phoenix thought they'd done their worst, they had turned the tables again. He saw Adams tapping a leather wallet just like the one he was holding. Somehow they had made a switch.

'Well,' said Aegeus, suspicion written into every wrinkle of his tired old face. 'May I see this proof?'

Phoenix's mind was thrown into tumult. If he produced the head, anyone who saw it would die. A grotesque picture burst into his imagination, of the boy-hero turning to stone before the entire gathering. Even worse, of an entire court destroyed, and with it any hope of completing the mission.

But how was this done? Phoenix met the eyes, the burning eyes, of Medea, and he remembered Adams' boasts. This sorcery was her work. He exchanged glances with Laura. This time there was nothing she could do. She was all out of ideas. It was time to turn the tables.

179

'Great Aegeus, I understand that my arrival must be of concern to your wife, the queen. After all, it is her son who stands to lose a throne. The wallet is hers.'

Seeing the look of shock on Medea's face, he felt his power growing. In a bolder, more assured voice, he addressed her. 'Lady Medea, would you examine the proof?'

He handed the wallet to the startled queen. She stared panic-stricken at the heavy leather bag. It was the turn of her flesh to crawl at the macabre trophy inside.

'I—'

Her eyes met those of Phoenix. The hatred burned stronger than ever. She knew she had been outwitted. Closing her eyes, she rested a hand on each of the wallets. Phoenix felt the charge of a strange power in the air. Her magic was doing its work. She had switched the wallets again. Unfastening the drawstring, Medea emptied the sword-hilt and sandals on the table.

The score bracelet chattered reassuringly.

Raising his goblet in triumph, Phoenix toasted Aegeus. 'To you, King and father.'

'By the gods of great Olympus!' cried Aegeus. 'It's true. You *are* my son.'

He stared at the sandals and sword-hilt then at the goblet in Phoenix's hand.

'No!' he cried. 'Don't drink.'

He rushed to dash the cup from Phoenix's hand.

'The drink is poisoned. I thought you were an imposter. I swear to you, my boy, this was the queen's doing. She told me you were a lying knave, come to kill me.'

Phoenix let him dash the cup with its harmless liquid to the floor. It was part of the legend, after all, so why deny the old man his place in it? As the king embraced him, Phoenix looked across at Adams. He made a suitable son for Medea. He shared her thirst for malice. His eyes burned with the same hatred.

4

As the morning mists cleared from the port of Athens next day, Phoenix found himself standing among a great crowd. It had been a night of rejoicing. Aegeus had embraced him as his rightful heir, Prince Theseus of Athens. Phoenix had come through, he'd played his part to the full. He was the toast of the entire city. Fires had been lit on every altar in all the temples of the city. Images of the gods had been heaped with gifts. The air was still filled with acrid smoke where oxen had been slaughtered and roasted in sacrifice to Olympus. Now the citizens of Athens jostled for a place at the harbour. There remained one last ceremony to perform. The banishment of a traitor. Two ships were being prepared at the quayside. The death ship to Crete and the ship of exile – Medea's ship.

'Queen Medea,' said Aegeus. 'You have shared my life, but you are now a proven traitor. You have been found guilty of the vilest treason. You have tried to poison Theseus, my first-born son and rightful heir to the throne of Athens. You tried to poison my mind against him, telling me he was a spy. Or, worse still, an assassin. Do you have anything to say before you are cast out?'

Medea and Adams were standing together, under armed guard.

'You old fool,' Medea said, her voice crackling with fury. 'Who are you to banish me? My power is greater by far than yours. I should have ruled here, not you. As for you, Theseus, relish your victory now because your fate is betrayal and black despair.'

Along the quayside, Laura flinched. The sorceress stood

181

proudly, her long hair flying in the wind. There wasn't a trace of shame.

'Hear me, Theseus. You are cursed. You and all who follow you.'

Aegeus shook his head sadly.

'I loved you Medea, as wife and queen . . . and mother to my son Medus.'

He looked at Adams, who turned his face away. He'd played the part long enough. He belonged to nobody but the spirit of evil that powered the game.

'Now I must lose you both.'

'You never had us,' raged Medea. 'With my spells I made you love me. You poor old fool, you were my puppet. That's all.'

Aegeus seemed to reel under the impact of her acid tongue.

'Enjoy your triumph Theseus,' shrieked Medea. 'But don't forget, another ship lies in this harbour, and when she sails she will carry the broken heart of Athens with her. Cast me out if you will, Aegeus, but you will never live to enjoy your new-found son. The Minotaur will avenge me.'

All eyes turned towards the black-sailed ship lying at anchor further along the quay. The celebrations of the night before seemed to evaporate. The death ship was ready to sail, bearing away fourteen of their sons and daughters. Aegeus waved to the crew of the first vessel that was to carry Medea into exile.

'Set sail. Convey this faithless witch across the sea. Begone, outcast.'

'Banish me then,' yelled Medea, flinging wide her arms. 'But hear this, Aegeus, there is no jail on Earth that can hold me, no shackles that can bind me. Circe, my mother, taught me the arts of mysteries of the sorcerers. I fly with the raven, swim with the shark, slither with the viper. Come the turn of the year the throne of Athens will be empty and you will be at the bottom of the sea. That's right, Aegeus, your broken body will be picked clean by the crabs, and I will return to set my son upon the throne.'

The ship carrying Medea was setting sail. But most of the

crowd were already turning their eyes towards the death ship. Aegeus led the procession to the black-sailed vessel.

'My heart is heavy this day,' said Aegeus. 'I have lost a queen and an heir. Now I must bid farewell to the flower of our youth.'

Laura was shuffling on to the ship. Phoenix knew what he had to do. His destiny lay in those endless, twisting passageways across the sea. He raised his voice against the wind.

'Wait! This cruel tribute has to end. Athens must no longer give up its children to die in the labyrinth.'

'What can we do?' asked Aegeus. 'It is the will of Zeus who delights in thunder. We dare not deny the dark-browed Lord of Olympus. Have you any idea what happened the last time we refused tribute? Famine and earthquake laid waste to the land. Our streets were littered with the dead. Would you have me bring the wrath of the gods down upon Athens a second time?'

'I am not talking about refusing tribute,' Phoenix told him. 'Let *me* be the tribute.'

He stepped forward and grabbed one of the youths boarding the ship.

'What's your name?'

'I am Themon.'

'Return to your family, Themon. I'm taking your place.'

'No, my son,' Aegeus cried, 'I cannot permit this sacrifice. What if you should perish?'

'Didn't I clear the coast of bandits?' Phoenix demanded, playing his part with gusto. 'Didn't I expose Medea as a sorceress and traitor?'

His mind was back in Seriphos and the exploits of which he couldn't boast. Didn't he destroy Medusa and the court of cruel Polydectes too?

'It is my destiny to face the beast in his lair. I must do this, or Athens will groan under the burden of her loss for generations to come.'

More importantly, Phoenix, Dad and Laura would be trapped in this savage world forever.

Aegeus conferred with his courtiers.

'Very well, you have my blessing for your adventure. But promise this, you must return safely to Athens.' He waved to his servants. 'Take this with you.'

They tossed a heavy bundle on to the deck of the ship.

'What is it?'

'A white sail. When you kill the beast, hoist it in place of this black one and I will know you're safe. I shall be atop that cliff waiting for you.'

He turned and beckoned a grey-haired man from the crowd. He was the priest of Poseidon, god of the sea. The priest washed his hands in a silver bowl and scattered grains of barley on the flames of a brazier. He raised his arms and shouted an order. 'Bring the offering.'

A bull, its great head swaying, was led on to the quay.

'Lord Poseidon, son of Cronus and Rhea, you who command the waves, grant safe passage to our sons and daughters and their safe return.'

Having slain the animal the priest cast some of its hair on the flames. Phoenix watched the spectacle for a few moments then walked towards Laura. Before he could reach her, he was alerted by a cry of dismay from the crowd.

'The queen has returned. Look! It's Medea!'

In the billowing smoke above the sacrificial flame, the witch-queen's features were forming.

The crowd fell back in terror.

'Cowardly Athens. You retreated from the armies of Minos the Conqueror. Now fall back before my wrath. Gaze upon your sons and daughters for you will never see them again. Soon, they will be as dead as the crew of this ship of exile.'

Aegeus stepped forward but she cut him short.

'Yes, you too Aegeus, bid farewell to your son. You wish to know his fate? Then watch.'

Sparks showered from her eyes and fell upon the carcass of the bull where it lay. New life breathed into the dead body and it began to rise. But a terrible transformation was occurring.

Rising man-like on two legs, the bull's haunted eyes sought out Phoenix.

'Look upon this creature,' cried Medea. 'Tremble at the Minotaur's strength. Fear him for he will soon crush your bones and feast on your broken flesh.'

In an instant she was gone and the bull was once more lying dead on the ground.

'Don't go,' Aegeus begged.

'I have to,' Phoenix told him. 'It's my destiny.'

As they prepared to set sail, he confided in Laura.

'My destiny,' he repeated. 'And my nightmare.'

The nightmare came that night. Phoenix's courage failed again. This time there were other faces in the darkness. Not just Laura. Danaë was there, Aegeus too. All trusting him. All betrayed by him.

But I didn't fail! I didn't betray anybody!

Then in the dream-haze, Dad turned to face him, not the twinkling-eyed John Graves who had been so excited about *The Legendeer*. This was his ghost. His eyes were dead, drained of life. His freckled skin was bleached and cold.

'You betrayed me,' he groaned. 'And you will betray them too.'

And Phoenix was screaming, screaming until the sunlight filtered between his eyelids and he caught sight of the black sail billowing overhead.

'Phoenix.'

The scream went on and on.

'Phoenix, wake up.'

His eyes filled with Laura's face, staring down at him.

'The nightmare?' she asked.

Of course it was the nightmare. It was never going to let go. She sat beside him on the deck of the ship. A seagull wheeled overhead, eerily echoing Phoenix's scream.

'Are you ready for this, Phoenix? Are you sure you can kill the beast?'

'I don't know.'

185

'You're thinking about Medea's curse, aren't you?'

'That,' Phoenix replied. 'And Dad.'

He shuddered at the dead-eyed John Graves who had accused him in his dream.

'I still don't get it,' Laura sighed. 'What is going on here? It doesn't make any sense.'

'I know,' said Phoenix. 'Sometimes I think this is just a game. But no computer program could be this real. Or this evil. We're in another world. We must be.'

'And it's a world we're going to get out of,' Laura said defiantly.

Phoenix hung his head. 'Are you sure about that?'

Laura looked impatient with him for a moment. Then her face came to life.

'I almost forgot. It's the reason I came to wake you.'

'What is?'

'You'll have to see this for yourself.'

He followed her into the quarters below decks, where the rest of the ship's sad cargo were sleeping.

'Look.'

Phoenix examined all twelve sleeping passengers. No wonder Laura wanted to see.

'All of them!' he gasped.

Laura nodded.

'Every one.'

Phoenix continued to stare. It was true. They all bore the same mark. An owl tattoo.

'This *is* a real world,' he said. 'I've always known it. But there is an intelligence at work here. Reede, the Gamesmaster, the gods, call it what you wish, but this intelligence is playing with every one of us as if it were a game.'

Laura listened without a single interruption. He had spoken of an instinct, an inkling. Now it was growing into knowledge.

'Just think of it,' said Phoenix. 'Everybody's playing a part. I was Perseus, now I'm Theseus. Adams was Medus. What's more, the game never ends. Nothing has changed since the time of the legends, fifty, a hundred centuries ago. The people

186

of this world are condemned to play over and over again, for all time. They're frozen in an age of terror. But what if somebody decides they don't want to play any more? What if they want out?'

Laura frowned. 'Go on.'

'There was that lad in Deicterion. He refused and the game did something to him. Danaë tried to tell me something and she died the same way. And it's all got something to do with this tattoo. That's why nobody breaks free.'

He was interrupted by the captain.

'I hope you slept well,' he called. 'We've reached our destination.'

Laura and Phoenix were the first to scramble up on deck. The other passengers followed them to the ship's rail a couple of minutes later. They assembled along the bulwark, gazing at the coast of Crete.

'Look!' shouted one of the sailors. 'To starboard. One of Minos' warships.'

Phoenix watched the warship's oars slicing through the waves. It was coming to bring them into harbour.

My destiny is reaching out to me.

But the warship wasn't the only thing out at sea that day. The waters began to boil before them, turning blood red. The other passengers fell back in horror. Within moments the cause of the scarlet stain became obvious.

'Surprise surprise!'

Phoenix watched the scene as if he were witnessing a third funeral pyre.

'I'd been expecting him.'

His Nemesis was approaching. Riding a chariot, drawn by dolphins, Adams and Medea were closing in on the ship.

'So,' Medea said, 'here you are Theseus, hastening to your death.'

Now Phoenix could see why the sea had turned red. In the bloodied waters he began to make out human features. Faces appeared first, with eyes staring and lifeless just as Dad's had been in Phoenix's dream.

'It's me,' cried Laura. 'Me and—'

'I know,' Phoenix murmured. 'Every one of the fourteen human sacrifices.' He glanced at the others. 'All of you.'

But Medea hadn't finished yet. Dipping her hand into the gory soup, she pulled out a familiar head. Laura screamed. The other passengers fell to their knees.

'The prince!' they cried.

Phoenix could only look at the bold, young face as if he was looking in a distorted fairground mirror. He was staring at his own death mask.

Medea turned her chariot and headed for the shore.

'I'll take my leave of you now,' she shouted gaily. 'I want to make sure of a ringside seat. I want to watch your face as you die.'

Nobody spoke.

Not one of them.

Each was facing their destiny in their own way.

5

Within the hour they were standing on Cretan soil, seven youths and seven maidens, chained to one another. They were guarded by fourteen soldiers, each carrying a brightly-patterned ox-hide shield, a murderous-looking javelin and a sword. On the cliffs above there were as many archers testing their bowstrings. Minos was taking no risks with his tribute.

'All hail Lord Minos,' one of the soldiers cried suddenly. 'Great King, law-giver, conqueror of Megara, master of Athens.'

Phoenix felt the prick of a spearpoint in his back.

'Kneel craven Athenians, bow your heads before your lord.'

Laura bristled. 'Lord indeed. He isn't *my* lord.'

The protest earned her a brutal kick in the back which sent her sprawling to the ground. The incident was seen by a tall, bearded figure in maroon robes. Judging by the way the crowd divided to let him pass, it could only be one man – Minos himself.

'Is she giving you problems?' he asked the soldier.

'No Sire.'

Phoenix could see Laura's eyes flashing.

'Then why are you mistreating the prisoner so?'

'She was defiant. She refused to swear allegiance, Sire.'

Phoenix's heart turned over. She had slighted Minos, King of Crete, conqueror of Athens. She could be put to the sword on the spot.

'Hail, King Minos,' he declared, pushing forward as far as his chains allowed. 'The fault is not my friend's. I have encouraged her in her pride.'

189

'And you are?'

He was about to play his trump card, claiming special status as Theseus, Prince of Athens when a familiar voice broke in.

'He is Theseus of Troezen, the bandit slayer.'

'Why thank you, Medea,' said Minos. 'I take it you two know each other.'

Medea glared at Phoenix with her blazing eyes.

'Oh, we know each other, King Minos. The boy is responsible for my banishment.'

'Well, well,' said Minos, stroking his beard. 'Two royal visitors at my court. The gods have blessed me. They have indeed.' He turned to Laura. 'Get up girl. Save your proud gestures for the Minotaur.'

Phoenix stretched out a helping hand, but Laura was determined to get up by herself.

'Come here, Theseus,' Minos ordered. 'Let me look at you.'

Phoenix stood before the King.

'So you are the bandit slayer, the hero of Athens. Medea has recounted your exploits. I am impressed, young prince. And to have offered yourself as part of the tribute! I wonder, is it courage or madness?'

Phoenix had asked himself the same question a hundred times!

'This should be good sport, Theseus. Never has such noble blood quenched the thirst of the beast.'

Phoenix managed his own gesture of defiance. 'I did not come to satisfy the appetite of the beast, King Minos, but to slay it.'

A murmur ran through the crowd until it was cut short by a noise from beneath the earth. Below their feet the ground trembled with a terrible roar, half-animal, half-human. It sang of savagery, but of sadness too. In the darkness the beast awaited them.

'Tut tut, Theseus,' chuckled Minos. 'I fear you have upset our monstrous son.'

The roar had penetrated Phoenix's soul. He could feel his courage draining away.

190

'Now, Theseus, I am sure you are tired after your voyage. Let me conduct you to your chambers.'

Phoenix was about to follow when he remembered his companions.

'What of them?'

'Why, they will be held in the dungeons until—' His eyes twinkled. 'Until feeding time.'

Phoenix stopped short.

'Then I will share their quarters.'

'So an Athenian with spirit. Very well, you shall all enjoy chambers in my palace. I can afford to be generous.' He gave a knowing wink. 'Besides, it will only be for one night.'

Another roar from the demon prison below.

One night, then we meet face to face.

Laughter rippled through the crowd. Two voices laughed loudest and longest – those of Adams and Medea.

Minos was as good as his word. When he said they would enjoy chambers at the palace, he really did mean enjoy. Tables were set with cooked meats, wine, fruit, vegetables, bread and cheese.

'I feel like a turkey,' grumbled Laura. 'Being fattened up for Christmas.'

'Christmas?' Phoenix exclaimed. 'I wish we had that long.'

'The king said we had one more night. When *exactly* do we go to the labyrinth?'

Did she really want to know?

'Tomorrow, at dawn.'

Laura took the news calmly, but she was unable to finish her meal. Phoenix was trying to think of a way to comfort her when there was a loud knock at the door.

'Prisoners, be upstanding for His Highness Lord Minos, Great King, law-giver.'

Laura shook her head. 'Do they have to go through this rigmarole every time?'

Phoenix smiled.

'Yes, Laura, every time. The rules of the game.'

191

Minos walked in followed by the members of his court.

'Prince Theseus,' he said. 'Pardon me for interrupting your meal, your *final* meal, but I wanted you to meet my family and my court.'

Phoenix stood and approached the king.

'Let me introduce my wife, Queen Pasiphaë, my sons Catreus, Deucalion and Glaucus.' Minos paused. 'And the flower of my court, my daughter Ariadne.'

Phoenix felt a shudder of recognition. He felt Ariadne's eyes on his face, the same eyes he had seen the first time he played the game.

Minos stroked his daughter's hair. 'Sweet Ariadne. So fair, so *loyal*.'

The princess shuddered at his touch. But Minos took little notice. He was keen to say his piece.

'The Fates are cruel indeed, brave Theseus. The bandit-slaying Prince of Athens and the Princess of Crete. In another time this would have been a match made on Olympus, a marriage to unite our warring lands.'

The introductions ran on and on. Phoenix avoided Medea and Adams. As he approached the end of the line he was hard-pressed to stifle a yawn. Then Minos pulled a master stroke.

'Last but not least, great Daedalus.'

Phoenix turned, then snapped to attention.

'Da—'

It was Dad, but the familiar green eyes cut Phoenix short with a warning glare. No emotion, no embrace. They had to continue to play their parts.

Minos was in a hearty mood. 'I see you recognize the name of our wise friend.'

Flustered by Dad's presence, Phoenix stammered out a reply.

'Yes, Lord Minos, I know of Daedalus. Who doesn't? He is the talk of all Greece. Hail to you, great inventor and architect of the labyrinth.'

*Hail to you, **father**.*

'You seem excited, young Theseus,' said Minos, the corners

192

of his mouth twitching with a sly grin. 'You don't look like a man enjoying his last night on this Earth.'

At the King's words Phoenix's doubts returned. He found himself glaring at Adams and Medea and saw the cold smiles on their faces. What were they up to?

Laura joined him and glanced at Minos and his courtiers. 'What is this?' she whispered. 'Do they have to watch us eat?'

Phoenix was about to reply when Ariadne detached herself from the rest of her party. She wandered around the room, finally drawing close to Phoenix. As she passed, a tiny piece of paper dropped from her sleeve and landed beside him. A sudden joy flowed through him. How could he have forgotten the legend? Ariadne would be there with sword and twine, helping him. She would be their salvation.

The myth is a pole star to navigate my way.

'Let them have their fun,' Phoenix told her, reassured by the meeting with Ariadne and Dad – or should it be Daedalus? 'We're going to have the last laugh.'

It was late and the court of Minos had left. While the lights were being extinguished in the corridor and the guard changed, Laura made her way to Phoenix's side.

'What was all that about earlier? How are we going to have the last laugh?'

'Remember what Pan always said, Laura? *Use the myth as the pole star to navigate your way.*'

Laura gave him an indulgent smile.

'I'm not likely to forget, am I?'

'Remember Princess Ariadne?'

'Mmm, what's she? The love interest?'

Laura seemed a bit nettled. So, she'd noticed the princess. Not jealousy, surely?

'I suppose she is actually,' Phoenix replied, enjoying teasing her. '*For the purposes of the game.*'

'Mmm.'

Laura *was* bothered.

Phoenix produced the note that Ariadne had slipped to him. Laura was determined not to be impressed. She barely raised an eyebrow.

'What is it?'

'I'm sure you've guessed already. The part of the story I'd almost forgotten.'

Maybe he'd been too paralyzed with fear by the prospect of returning to the labyrinth to remember.

'Ariadne falls in love with Theseus.'

Laura rolled her eyes.

'Of course she does.'

'Oh, stop it. This is good news, Laura. It's the most famous part of the legend. The labyrinth has been constructed as an impossible maze. Daedalus made it that way. But between them Ariadne and Daedalus come up with a plan to save Theseus and his companions. That's what the note says. They're coming. Soon.'

'Daedalus? You mean your dad?'

Phoenix nodded.

'So answer me this. If he can rescue us now, why didn't he do something earlier?'

'I don't know,' Phoenix admitted, as images of their previous flight in the labyrinth started to trouble him. 'The important thing is, they're planning a rescue.'

'Let me guess, a helicopter.'

'Now you're just being silly. No, it has to follow the rules of the game. In the legend Ariadne gives Theseus a ball of twine and a sword. Theseus ties the twine to the door of the labyrinth and plays it out behind him. He uses the sword to kill the beast and follows the thread back to the entrance.'

He was buzzing with excitement, but Laura wasn't so sure.

'I don't know. Remember how hard it was to defeat Medusa. You've said yourself that the Minotaur was too strong for you. I mean, how many times have you run from it?'

'I'm not running any more,' said Phoenix. 'This time I intend to win.'

'What's changed?'

194

'This, for one,' said Phoenix, waving the points bracelet under her nose. 'We've built up a huge score. I'll win this time. I know it.'

'But what if it's a trick?' Laura asked. 'We can't expect anybody to bail us out. Not the architect, and not a lovesick princess. No, it's just too sudden, too convenient.'

Phoenix was furious with her. He'd been so happy. He'd convinced himself that they were almost home. How could she doubt him? Didn't she realize? He *was* the Legendeer. He stormed to the window in a fit of pique and stared out across the sea. Was it too much to expect your best friend to believe in you?

'I've been patient with you, Laura, but I've got to say it. You don't know what you're talking about.'

He was about to tell her a few more home truths when he heard footsteps echoing below him. By the torches on the battlements he was able to make out a band of soldiers marching two chained prisoners away. A new horror clawed at his insides.

'No, this is impossible.'

But there they were, caught in the torchlight from Minos' palace, the princess and the architect. It was them, Dad and Ariadne, accompanied by four guards.

'What is it, Phoenix?'

'Dad and Ariadne. They're being taken away under guard. I don't understand. They can't be. They're the ones who are supposed to help us.'

He wracked his brains, trying to make sense of it. His hands flew up to his face, tugging at his skin, as a fever of panic ran through him. Now he was stammering, as if begging Laura to make everything right.

'The legend's clear. Ariadne falls in love with Theseus. She enlists the help of Daedalus. The string . . . the sword . . . I'm not dreaming. Laura, that's the way it is, the way it has to be. It's the only way we can hope to complete the game.'

Loud laughter filled the room. Phoenix and Laura turned to see the far wall bulging, becoming molten and fluid. Two faces

195

emerged, familiar faces, Adams and Medea. The laughter was louder now, it circled them like a pack of hyenas.

'The way it *should* be,' cackled Medea. 'The way it would have been if I hadn't had a word in the ear of King Minos. Forget all those things you heard in Athens, my prince. He is a sweetie, really, old Minos. He would do anything for a sorceress in need.'

'You mean—'

'My dear Theseus, you don't think I would allow an interfering girl to upset my plans, do you? Poor little Ariadne, she's no match for me. Or that dried-up fool Daedalus. Haven't you grown out of happy endings yet? It's been fun watching your silly face light up with joy, thinking you were saved, then seeing the dawn of realization, that you're going to die all the same.'

'You witch!'

Medea purred like a cat.

'Thank you for the kind compliment, Theseus. Goodnight, sweet prince. Sleep tight. I am trusting you to provide us with some fine sport tomorrow. Put up a good fight, just so long as you lose.'

As the faces faded from the wall, Adams yelled his parting shot.

'The game is up Theseus. Or should I say *Phoenix*? Ariadne and Daedalus locked away where they can't interfere. All hope gone. The will of the gods is done. Surprise, surprise.'

6

Beyond the screen, in that old world once more frozen in time, the voice in the machine was speaking its impenetrable code.

The will of the gods is done. Poor, poor Phoenix expecting me to play fair. To think, you really expected Ariadne to come along with her string and sword. Not this time, Legendeer. This myth-world is faithful in every detail to the tales you love. As you put it yourself, a universe frozen in time, playing out the old truths again and again. But it is still **my** *myth-world, and these creatures are my subjects, my pawns to be moved as I wish. Now tremble before my power, Legendeer, for I am the angel of death come to pass over your house and your world. I know now that it is no accident you came into my world. We are bound together, you and I, champions of our savage gods. Two sides of destiny's coin. Then let us flip and see which of us finishes this game face up.*

Christina Graves meanwhile watched her son trying to sleep. She longed to reach out and touch his cheek. If the pain of loss she felt for her husband was sharp, this agony was worse still. To see her son going through such ordeals and be unable to help him, it was the most terrible torture she could suffer. Unable to tear herself away from the screen, she had barely eaten in days. She felt light-headed, her mind switching from one thing to another as she tried to make sense of what was happening to her family. From time to time, she flicked through Uncle Andreas' journal, continually rereading his story. She ached to hear the dead man's voice, echoing down the years. She traced his descent into hell as he saw the

197

demons beating at the door of his world and was labelled as a madman for trying to raise the alarm. But the section she pored over longest was the one about his headaches. The part where he believed he suffered *because he had been born in the wrong world*.

That was it. All these years, the family had closed their eyes to the truth.

Andreas had been right all along. There was another world, maybe many worlds. But life there danced to a different, more macabre tune. Time didn't run foward generation after generation, it seemed to turn in an endless loop. Man and monster alike, they were condemned to wage an endless struggle, waiting for time to start again.

Then Christina understood. There was a way for time to continue its forward march.

'Oh, sweet heavens,' she murmured.

Because that way was to break out of the myth-world altogether and continue the struggle in this one.

Sleep was hard to come by, at least for Laura and Phoenix. They talked in hushed tones until the early hours, but in the end even Laura was lying curled up – restless and tossing it's true – but sleeping nonetheless. As for their twelve companions, they had fallen asleep immediately. They had even slept through the appearance of Adams and Medea. Phoenix found himself padding across the room, examining the owl tattoo that they all bore. Could that explain the depth of their sleep? It was a blessing, of course. At least they didn't have to dream and live out the terror in the tunnels below.

He grimaced despite himself. 'It's no dream now. It's real.'

All hope gone. Somewhere in the bowels of the palace, two people lay chained, the only two people in the world who could have helped him, the princess and the architect. Phoenix raised his eyes to greet the first glimmerings of dawn. Smoke was rising from the kitchens as the servants prepared breakfast for the court. He watched it plume heavenward and he remembered the funeral pyre on the beach at Seriphos.

When the bird had come, when he'd been given renewed hope.

'Gone,' he said with a sigh.

Discouraged and weary, Phoenix leaned his back against the wall and slid down to the floor. There he rested with his head on his knees.

'So what's left?'

In answer to his question, an unwelcome guest entered the room. Phoenix turned his face to the wall.

'What's this, Legendeer?' asked Pan. 'Aren't you happy to see your old friend?'

'Friend? You're no friend. You serve *him*, the Gamesmaster.'

'I serve the greatest power. I serve that force which can break out of this timeless prison.'

Phoenix turned his eyes towards Pan.

'You serve evil.'

'I serve life,' Pan retorted. 'When you and your kind are just memories, this thing you call evil will still be there. Andreas' blood runs in your veins all right. You're a sentimental fool just like him.'

'So you did visit him?'

'I tried. *We* tried. But the wall between the worlds was too strong. There was no way to pass through. My kind could only appear to him as shadows of ourselves, ghosts if that's what you want to call us. Then we found the magic that could thin the walls to breaking point.'

'The game!' cried Phoenix. 'You mean the game, don't you?'

Pan nodded gravely.

'A strange irony, isn't it, that this computer, this buzzing box, this highest point of your technology and science, the discovery that made you *civilized*, it's the very thing that will set free our power. Your computers, the most complex machines you have invented, they will open the gates to us. Then your world, your smug, flabby world will be ours.'

Phoenix stared in horror at his tormentor.

'You won't be hearing from me again,' said Pan. 'Destiny awaits you. Listen.'

In response to his words, a key scraped in the lock. Soldiers marched into the room, stirring the beast's victims.

Phoenix knew what was left.

Death.

Medea and Adams followed the soldiers into the room. They watched the reddish glow of the dawn spreading across the mosaic floor around the fourteen Athenians.

'What's the matter?' Adams asked sarcastically. 'Something bothering you, *Theseus*?'

The captain had no time for pointless banter. 'Look lively. The Minotaur's getting restless. He wants his breakfast.'

'Yes,' said Adams triumphantly. 'And guess who's the first course.'

Within minutes they were moving downwards, always downwards, negotiating a stone staircase into the stinking darkness. Phoenix felt the cloying, musty heat of the labyrinth. His nightmare was rushing up to meet him.

'Are you all right, Phoenix?'

He gave Laura a nod, but his heart was thudding and his knees seemed to buckle at every step. In the Gorgon's cave it had been Laura who had gone faint with terror. Now it was Phoenix's turn. He was walking on legs that were so rubbery and so weak they could hardly support him.

How can I face my destiny? I don't have the courage.

'All hail King Minos!' barked the captain of the guard as they reached the bottom of the last and steepest flight of stairs. 'Bow your heads, Athenians.'

While Phoenix and Laura's twelve companions sank obediently to their knees before the King, they stood upright, looking straight ahead. A few well-aimed kicks at the back of their knees and the two friends were also forced to kneel.

'Still defiant, Prince?' asked Minos. 'We'll see how your Athenian pride serves you in there.' He stabbed a finger in the direction of the labyrinth.

'I've seen this show of bravery before, remember. That's

right, the others were like you, breathing fire as they stood at this door. But once they got in there—'

He rapped loudly at the metal-studded wooden door, stirring the Minotaur deep in his lair. 'Oh, they sing a different tune then.'

Minos bent, bringing his face close to Phoenix's, then repeating the operation for Laura's benefit.

'I've heard them begging, screaming, whimpering. Yes, even the strongest of them.'

Laura scrambled to her feet.

'You're no king,' she cried. 'You're a monster.'

'No, my dear, the monster is in here.'

It was almost time. The entourage of King Minos was filling the area outside the labyrinth. Medea and Adams were there, hungry for sport. But Minos still had one surprise in store.

'Before you leave us, brave prince, perhaps you wish to bid farewell to your only friends at this court.'

He gestured to his guards and Dad and Ariadne were brought forward, struggling and resisting.

'Such good timing, don't you think? Here they are, freshly returned from their short stay in my dungeons. Such loyal friends to their sovereign.'

Phoenix managed a smile for the architect and the princess.

'How touching!' Medea chimed in gleefully.

'Yes,' Adams agreed. 'It's enough to bring a tear to my eye.'

'Let me go too,' Dad cried. 'My place is with them.'

Minos gave a smile of satisfaction. 'So, you want to die together. Why not?'

But before Dad could join Phoenix, Minos had a parting gift. He raised his sceptre and pressed it to the prisoner's throat. It sizzled like a brand. When Minos removed it, the tell-tale owl tattoo was left imprinted on the throat of John Graves.

'That's just in case you should escape the Minotaur,' said Minos.

'Escape the Minotaur,' Medea repeated, to raucous laughter. 'What an imagination you have, Sire.'

201

Still wincing from the pain, Dad joined Phoenix and Laura, and they walked slowly towards the door. The captain of the guard was jangling his bunch of keys, searching for the one that would unlock the nightmare. He turned the key.

'Ready, Sire.'

The guards were prodding the Minotaur's victims forward at swordpoint when Adams rushed forward and whispered a parting taunt in Phoenix's ear.

'How do you stop a bull charging, Phoenix?' His eyes twinkled. 'Why, cut up his credit card, of course.'

Phoenix tried to throw a punch but missed, falling against the guard holding Ariadne. She reacted quickly, snatching the soldier's sword and handing it to Phoenix. He looked into her dark eyes and smiled.

The legend may yet run its true course.

The disarmed guard tried to snatch back his weapon, but Minos called him back.

'Let him have the tooth-pick,' he chuckled. 'For all the good it will do against the beast.'

Phoenix closed the fingers of his right hand around the sword's hilt and felt the reassurance of cold steel. The great door slammed behind him and he stumbled into the gloom, feeling the walls slimy against his left palm. As he searched for the others, he heard the sound he'd dreaded for so long. The key was turning again, locking them inside the labyrinth.

'Phoenix?'

It was Laura's voice.

'Over here.'

It was quiet in the maze, the silence as complete as the blackness of the tunnels.

'I'm shaking.'

He felt for Laura's hand. She was as cold as ice.

'Me too,' Phoenix whispered.

'Just try not to let it show,' said Dad, joining them. 'They want us to put on a show. They want to hear us beg for our lives. Don't give them the satisfaction.'

The beast shattered the silence with an earth-shaking roar. He was beginning to move, his bull's hooves thudding monotonously through the tunnels.

'This way,' said Dad. 'Everybody, this way.'

'Are you sure he knows what he's doing?' Laura whispered to Phoenix.

'I'm not sure of anything.'

They reached a meeting of the ways. There were four openings.

'Now where?'

The beast's roar echoed down the gallery they'd just left.

'As far from that as we can get.'

Phoenix and Dad were leading the group into a shaft which sank quite steeply downward.

'They're leading us to the beast,' cried one of the youths suddenly. 'How do we know we can trust them?'

'Please,' begged Laura. 'We have to do as they say.'

Phoenix leaned forward and whispered in Dad's ear.

'Where have you been?'

'I've been in Minos' dungeons,' Dad replied. 'That's where Glen Reede treated me to a full account of his plans.'

'You've met him! But he doesn't exist.'

'I know. Put it this way, I met the spirit that goes by his name, the Gamesmaster. He treated me to a computer link-up, a kind of e-mail written on the air.'

It was Laura's turn to quiz him. 'So what does he want?'

Phoenix already knew, but he let Dad tell his tale.

'The usual stuff you get from madmen. Conquest. World domination. Do you know what I and all the others on the team have been designing? A two-way door. Think about it, if we can go into the game, then why can't the game come out to us?'

As Phoenix remembered Pan's words, Laura stared in disbelief.

'That's right. How did he put it? Yes. *In a few months every teenager on the planet will be playing **The Legendeer**. Each individual will face his or her own personal Armageddon. One* *minute some wretched teenager will be slaying demons, the next the real thing will be there in his bedroom.'*

Suddenly, Phoenix could see it all in his mind's eye. The two worlds, the thinning wall, the numbers that were more than a series of coded messages – they were an entry code.

'There's going to be a games console in every room,' said Dad, trying to come to terms with what he had heard. 'The game is so convincing everybody will want to play. Think what this means. This will be unlimited terror, a war of annihilation waged from inside your own home. Reede's created a fifth column of demons to destroy us from within.'

Laura's voice was shaking. 'And this is possible?'

Dad looked around at the labyrinth.

'Are you going to tell me it isn't?'

'Dad,' said Phoenix. 'I hope you've got a plan.'

'Oh, I've got a plan all right,' Dad answered. 'If the Minotaur gives us enough time to carry it through.'

'What have you got in mind?' Phoenix asked, but the frightened youth interrupted Dad's reply.

'No,' he shouted, his voice hysterical with fright. 'I won't do it. It's this way. Who's with me?'

One girl detached herself from the group.

'I don't trust the Prince, either.'

Without another word, the frightened pair disappeared down a third tunnel, the only one of the four which was glimmering with light.

'Come back,' cried Dad.

'He's right,' said Phoenix. 'It's a trap. The light's only there to make you think there's a way out.'

'It's no use, Phoenix,' Laura told him gently. 'They're beside themselves with terror. You can't stop them.'

The group were edging forward, starting occasionally at the ear-splitting bellowing that seemed to burst out of the darkness like a cannon going off.

'They were right,' bleated another of their companions. 'We're walking into danger. I wish I'd gone with the others.'

'Don't be a fool,' Phoenix snapped. 'We've got to stick together.'

He had barely finished speaking when the darkness erupted with the shrieks and screams of the pair who had broken ranks. Amid their desperate shouts and cries came the sound of gurgling, of throats filling with blood. The beast had them now.

'There,' Phoenix told the group. 'That's what happens if we strike out on our own. We have to trust . . . Daedalus.'

'That's it,' said Dad, admiring his son's quick thinking. 'Play the game to the end.'

'But where are we going?' asked Phoenix. 'Is this it – the bomb for Glen Reede?'

Dad nodded. 'Remember the cheats?'

'Yes?'

'Well, I think that terminal is the key. It led us home once. We've just got to find it. Then it's my turn to play. As you said, a bomb for Glen Reede.'

'You do what you have to,' said Phoenix, certain of his destiny at last. 'I'll handle the Minotaur.'

They had edged forward another twenty or thirty paces when a shaft of light blazed unexpectedly into the maze.

'Enjoying yourself, my prince?' asked Medea, her mink-dark eyes fixing him. 'And what's this, there are fewer of you now. Dear me, how careless.'

There was sobbing in the gloom behind him. The youth who had been complaining earlier rushed forward and threw himself to his knees under the grating.

'Please,' he begged in a quavering voice. 'Don't leave us here to die.'

He pointed an accusing finger at Laura, Phoenix and Dad.

'They're the ones to blame, not us. Let the Minotaur have them instead.'

And Phoenix was angry. Angry because he remembered the dream when he'd been paralyzed by fear. Angry because he remembered begging to get out. Angry because he could see so much of himself in this whining youth. But I've been changing, he told himself. Now the transformation must be complete.

From zero to hero.

'Get up,' Phoenix ordered. 'It won't do you any good.'

'That's right,' said Medea. 'It won't. But it's so much fun to watch.'

A rush of footfalls in the darkness, heavy, cloven hooves clopping close behind them, and it wasn't Pan.

'Come on,' Dad urged. 'This way. Quickly.'

They were running too, their breath spilling out in tortured gasps. The roaring of the beast seemed more distant now.

'Get your breath back,' Phoenix told them in hushed tones. 'And don't say a word. We have to listen, try to work out where he is.'

'What's the point?' came a desperate reply. 'He'll get us anyway. There's no way out, not for any of us.'

Phoenix wanted to knock the words back down the lad's throat. He confined himself to a sharp retort. 'That's enough!'

Phoenix was listening, trying to discover the whereabouts of the Minotaur, when Laura drew him aside.

'What are we doing, Phoenix? If we carry on like this, it's just a matter of time before it finds us.'

'Don't you think I know that? Dad, there isn't much time.'

'This way. It's round the next corner.'

They reached the silver tetrahedron with its bull's head symbol. Just as Phoenix was daring to hope, Dad spoke, chilling him to the core.

'Now,' he said, producing a razor-sharp knife. 'You must cut my throat.'

206

7

'You want me to do what?' cried Phoenix, horrified.

'I've had it with them,' gasped the panic-stricken youth who'd been thinking of running. He was appalled by what he'd just heard. 'I'll find my own way out.'

The sound of running feet echoed through the maze. Two, maybe three of the group were following him, fleeing through the passageways. Dad looked sadly after them, then gripped Phoenix by both arms.

'You saw what Minos did to me.'

He drew back the collar of his tunic to expose the owl tattoo.

'Now stop arguing, Phoenix. You know what this is. If any of Reede's pawns resists he destroys them with this. You have to cut it out quickly or I'm dead.'

'Cut it out? But are you sure that'll work?'

'Who knows? But I have to try. If I don't do anything, I'm a dead man.'

Before Phoenix could argue any more, a second chorus of shrieks was crashing round the walls of the labyrinth, followed by more grunting and bellowing. More death.

Laura was speaking again, breathless and concerned:

'Phoenix, we're depending on you. Do it.'

'Do it,' ordered Dad, forcing the knife on Phoenix. 'Now. Before anybody sees what we're doing.'

Another roar, louder than ever. The beast was going for the kill. A hidden door flew open behind them, timber splintering, dust showering them, and shards of metal flying through the air, pricking and slicing at skin. It was there, right among them.

Phoenix was going to face his destiny.

'Laura,' he shouted. 'You've got to help Dad. I'll try to keep the Minotaur off.'

Phoenix sensed Dad and Laura in the stifling darkness, their love. It was a bond of steel. There was still hope. It gave him the strength to face his nightmare.

'Let me see you,' he shouted.

The beast's hands were clawed and covered in tough, wiry hair. Phoenix felt the brush of its thick, impossibly powerful fingers and his flesh shrank in panic from its touch. It blundered blindly past him, pacing, searching for signs of life. Finding none, it resumed its hunt, its hooves thudding dully in the dark.

'Laura,' Phoenix hissed. 'How are you doing?'

'Nearly got it,' she said. 'It's an implant, just under the skin. Fortunately, it's shallow.'

The survivors of the beast's attacks were cowering behind them and nobody was protesting any more. The fate of the others had put an end to all resistance. It was an obedience dictated by terror.

Hurry up, Laura.

The roaring of the Minotaur began again, right behind them.

'Laura?'

'Done!'

Phoenix saw her fingers on the knife. Dad appeared, holding a blood-stained cloth to his neck.

'Now,' he said. 'Time to put an end to this.'

But the words were no sooner out of his mouth than the hot, stinking breath of the beast blasted into Phoenix's face.

'Get back,' screamed Laura.

'Not this time,' said Phoenix. 'I'm done with running. It's time to make a stand.'

He grasped the hilt of the sword.

'How do you stop a bull charging? Answer. You cut up his credit card. And everything else!'

The Minotaur was so close he could see its yellow eyes, the

black muzzle, the razor teeth in the mighty, grinding jaws. Gathering the survivors behind him, Phoenix lashed out with the blade, tearing through skin and hair. Phoenix felt the welcome pulse of the score bracelet.

'Keep it off,' cried Dad.

He had pulled something from the lining of his tunic, the size of a coin. It was a miniature CD.

'The bomb?' asked Phoenix.

Dad nodded.

'A computer virus. If I'm right, we will have about a minute to escape through the terminal before it begins to work and closes the gate for ever.'

Phoenix nodded. All he had to do was to give Dad time to use it.

'Let's finish this,' he said.

The Minotaur grasped its weapon, the giant, studded club. As Phoenix crouched, facing the beast, Dad ran to the wall. His fingers were trying to prise open a panel on the terminal.

'Come on,' he cried to the others. 'This will fit in here somewhere.'

The Minotaur made its move, rushing them, swinging the club in huge arcs, dislodging bricks from the walls and uprooting stones from the floor.

'It's no good,' yelled Laura, tugging at the panel. 'It won't budge.'

The club was swinging again, forcing Phoenix to flatten himself against the wall, then again, making him throw himself flat on the floor.

As the beast lumbered forward, he rolled across the slimy paving. He could see spots of the Minotaur's blood in the puddles. But it didn't terrify him. Enranged by the sword-cut, it was flailing about without purpose.

'Try again, Laura!' cried Dad. 'This is definitely a terminal. It's the connection between the ancient powers and modern technology. This disc will fit somewhere. It's got to.'

The club swung, the downdraft brushing Phoenix's face.

Now for the death blow, he told himself preparing to strike.

'We've tried everywhere,' groaned Laura.

'Keep going,' Dad panted, refusing to give in.

Phoenix slashed with the sword, cutting the beast on the arm. Driven mad with pain, it staggered into a corner. But just as Phoenix raised his sword in a two-handed grip, ready to deliver the final blow an arrow struck the hilt of the sword, slicing through the skin between Phoenix's thumb and finger.

As Phoenix crashed against the wall, the sword spun from his hand.

'Mr Graves!' screamed Laura. 'I think I've got it.'

Meanwhile, Phoenix was crawling across the floor, slithering away from the club, grasping for the sword. The club struck him a glancing blow, impacting muscle and bone. He was on his knees, pain coursing down his left side.

'Yes, that's it,' yelled Dad, momentarily oblivious to the peril facing his son. 'That's it!'

The beast had Phoenix. Twisting its fingers through his tunic, it lifted him off the floor and snorted its hatred into his face.

That's when Phoenix heard a weapon hissing through the air. He saw it flash in the half-light. His sword. In Laura's hands. Phoenix was twisting and turning in the Minotaur's grasp, trying to win enough time for her to strike. The beast was staring at him, as if seeing something of itself in Phoenix, his human part. There was no bellowing now, just a hoarse snorting as the beast examined Phoenix's face.

'Now, Laura!'

But still she didn't strike. Phoenix was dangling in the beast's clutches.

This is it; my nightmare, but I didn't run. I stayed. I fought.

Maybe I have to die, Phoenix thought. But at least I wasn't a coward. I've stopped running.

Half expecting the Minotaur to finish him, he closed his eyes and yelled out a desperate plea. 'Laura!'

She stabbed with the sword, hard into the Minotaur's thigh but she couldn't force the blade through the dense slabs of muscle. The beast roared nonetheless. As it twisted to face its attacker, Laura hacked at its ankles. Stung by the unexpected blows, the beast reeled round, releasing Phoenix. One great fist sent the entire group of Athenians tumbling like skittles. Staggering over to Laura, Phoenix closed his hand round the hilt.

How do you stop a bull charging?

'Face me, beast!'

Weary from its wounds, the Minotaur staggered.

'The gate's open,' shouted Dad. 'We can get through.'

Phoenix felt his destiny intense within him and lunged at the Minotaur. Driving the blade upwards and inwards, he felt it grate against the beast's ribs. Then the huge body sagged and its eyes misted over.

Curling backwards, it fell heavily where so many of its victims had fallen before.

'Dead?' asked Laura.

Phoenix stood over the massive frame of the Minotaur.

'Dying.'

He saw bewilderment and pain in its yellow eyes, then the long sigh as they closed.

'It's over.'

Dad was waving them towards the terminal, now transformed into a shimmering gateway back home.

'Come on, you two. We've won.'

'That's right,' came a girl's voice. 'You've won. Now go from this terrible place while you can.'

Ariadne was looking down at him through a grating.

'Come with us,' said Phoenix.

'I can't. You have to leave me behind. It's the legend – my destiny. I belong here.'

'Are you sure?'

'I'm sure.'

Phoenix returned her smile.

We've won.

But he'd counted without Adams. Phoenix glimpsed him out of the corner of his eye, drawing his bow.

'Surprise, surprise.'

The arrow sang in the stale air before hitting the brickwork, just a hair's breadth from Phoenix's head.

'How did you get in here?'

'Have you forgotten the strength of Medea's magic?'

Having loosed his last arrow, Adams drew his sword. He appeared possessed, stabbing and slashing in a blood rage, his features contorted in hatred. Two sounds filled the passageways, the clash of swords as Phoenix met him blade to blade, and the rush of air through the gateway.

Dad and Laura were already inside the gate, holding out their hands.

'Come on, Phoenix.'

But Adams wouldn't accept defeat. What was left of his human side seemed to be shrivelling as he stormed forward, sword flashing. He belonged to the myth-world now. He was rapidly becoming a demon creature himself.

Phoenix was struggling to parry the onslaught, but there was the gateway between the worlds beckoning him. It was now or never. He could almost hear the virus doing its work. Phoenix mustered all his strength as he dashed the blade from Adams' hand and pushed him into them. As they staggered back, Phoenix cuffed his Nemesis across the face and tried to haul him into the gate by the scruff of the neck.

'You've had your fun,' he said. 'I thought death would be your punishment, but there's something worse. You're going to go back to being a small-town loser. You're going home.'

Phoenix glimpsed Ariadne in the background. In a moment of horror, he remembered the black sail. But it was too late. King Aegeus' part in the legend would remain unchanged. Grief-stricken, he would fall to his death.

Taking advantage of Phoenix's hesitation, Adams wrenched himself free and fell back into the myth-world. Like Phoenix, he had chosen his destiny. Then everything was fading, fading away. All Phoenix could see was the golden haze, and shimmering within it the numbers. The game dissolved around them and they were back in the study.

Level complete.

Game over.

Epilogue

Six weeks later, Phoenix was leading his way up a dusty path past an overgrown and neglected orange grove. He paused to take in his surroundings. For a brief moment his mind turned to Adams. For weeks, the police had been searching the woods and dragging the canals in the vain hope of finding some trace of him. But Phoenix soon dismissed thoughts of Adams and his distraught parents. There was nothing he could do for them, any of them. Behind him, through the heat haze, Phoenix could see the waters of the blue Aegean. He thought of a grief-stricken King and his resting place beneath the waves.

'How far now?' he asked.

'Just over that hill,' Mum replied.

'Thank goodness for that,' panted Dad, mopping his brow. 'I'm done in.'

But Phoenix was anything but. He broke into a run. In a few minutes, he would be there, in the garden of Uncle Andreas, where Pan had once stood.

'Don't expect too much,' Mum told him. 'it's been abandoned for years.'

'There has to be something,' shouted Phoenix. 'I've got to know what this is all about.' He could see the journal entry. The few devastating lines about the headaches.

The more I think about it, the sickliness, the band of pain, the strange waking fever that has been with me all my life, the more I realize that it has something to do with the ghosts. When they gather, when they step out of the shimmering light and speak to me, then I understand. I belong to their world.

214

I always have. For all time, I will be a stranger inside my own skin. I have a mission. For every ghost that believes in life and justice and warns me of the dangers of the gate, there are others who are filled with death and destruction. They are knocking at the door.

But they will not pass me. I am the Legendeer. My task is to keep the gate closed, to keep out the demon legions. Though it breaks my heart every day of my life, I will never give up my vigil. To leave my post would be to abandon this world to horror.

Phoenix looked back. 'I have to discover who I am.'

'Everybody said Uncle Andreas was a madman,' Mum had said, setting down the journals. 'He died without a soul believing him.'

But we believe you now, Andreas, thought Phoenix as he forced himself into a final sprint over the brow of the hill. Then there it was, the garden with its stone wall, and the house. It wasn't much to look at. The roof tiles had gone and the timbers were rotten. The front door had long since been smashed in. It was a picture of dereliction.

'There has to be something,' Phoenix said out loud.

With that, he stepped through the doorway. A few moments later, his parents arrived.

'Phoenix,' called Mum. 'Where are you?'

'Here. In the back room.'

Dad had finally caught up. 'Have you found anything?' he asked.

'Come and see.'

Then all three of them were standing in the room, stunned to silence. Painted on the walls were images of Pan, Medusa, and the Minotaur. But that wasn't all. All around them, scrawled in a frenzy were thousands of numbers, all multiples of three. The language of the computer game.

Hundreds of miles away, at that very moment, the Osibonas were completing their early evening routine at the Graves house, drawing the curtains and putting on the lights. A precaution against burglary while they were away. Laura paused for a moment in the study. If only her parents knew what she'd been through.

All that horror, all those demons, and as far as her parents were concerned, none of it had happened. Days of terror had flown by in a mere second of recorded time this side of the screen. So that was how things stood with Laura. Every day she stumbled through the usual routines, still hearing the snarl of madness from that other world, and all the while she had to keep her nightmares to herself. Laura shied away from touching anything. Though John Graves had destroyed the PR suits and the rest of the equipment, she was still wary of approaching the computer.

'Is it over?' she murmured out loud.

'What did you say, Laura?' asked Mrs Osibona.

'Nothing, Mum.'

'Hurry up, we're going now.'

'Coming.'

But as the Osibonas closed the front door behind them, the computer purred into life. By the time they were getting in the car, the very same sequences of numbers that Phoenix was reading on a whitewashed wall in Greece were flashing in this empty room back home. And as Mrs Osibona turned right on to the High Street, the numbers were racing across the screen, pulsating with menace.

So you think you've won, Legendeer? I may have abandoned my attempt to enter your world by the front door, but there are other ways in. Dozens of them. You think you're secure? You think your world is safe? Well, think again.

For every world like yours, for every planet spinning self-satisfied on its axis, there are five, ten, twenty myth-worlds. And they are not stories, Legendeer. They are real, as real as you are. Even now I am knocking at the door of another world like yours. And when I'm done there, when my demons have visited every home and plucked out their owners' hearts, then I will come for you.

216

Then, in the maelstrom of swirling numbers, the voice added its final warning:

You don't need to be asleep to have nightmares.

Vampyr Legion

What if there are real worlds where our night-mares live and wait for us?

Phoenix has found one and it's alive. Armies of bloodsucking vampyrs and terrifying were-wolves, the creatures of our darkest dreams, are poised to invade our world.

But Phoenix has encountered the creator of *Vampyr Legion*, the evil Gamesmaster, before and knows that this deadly computer game is for real – he must win or never come back.

Warriors of the Raven

The game opens up the gateway between our world and the world of the myths.

The Gamesmaster almost has our world at his mercy. Twice before fourteen-year-old Phoenix has battled against him in *Shadow of the Minotaur* and *Vampyr Legion*, but Warriors of the Raven is the game at its most complex and deadly level. This time, Phoenix enters the arena for the final conflict, set in the world of Norse myth. Join Phoenix in Asgard to fight Loki, the Mischief-maker, the terrifying Valkyries, dragons and fire demons – and hope for victory. Our future depends on him.